MW01128711

Nobody Wins

Nobody Wins

Nobody Wins

Nobody Wins

Acknowledgments

Many thanks to my family who was patient with me through this writing process, and to my brother Mike for working so tirelessly on the cover art. His talent amazes me.

Thanks to all of you who bought this book, and took a chance on this first-time writer.

Nobody Wins

by
Daniel Russo

"Book 1 of 2"

Nobody Wins

Nobody Wins

Nobody Wins

1

ETHAN MONROE OPENED HIS EYES to realize he had fallen asleep during his meeting. Luckily the meeting was for the whole company, so no one had noticed his sleeping. *How long have I been asleep?*
Ethan was a very smart man, but although he had much skill, his business wasn't doing well. One of the only other great business men in his company was Josh Anderson. He and Ethan

were great friends; they had formed an inseparable bond. The only thing they did not agree on was the fact Josh was a religious man.

Ethan was a plain man. He didn't believe in religion, period. He had a beautiful wife named Ruth, and the best daughter a man could ask for named Juliette.

Ethan sat at his desk filling out paper work and looking up how Comp City's numbers were doing, and how they could beat their opponent Best Deals. He walked out of his office to tell his secretary that he couldn't make the other meeting at 2:30 p.m. because it was his daughter's birthday.

His secretary's name was Mary. She was indispensable. Mary was the reason he was on time to meetings, the one that reminded him to sign his name on the last piece of paperwork, and so many things that helped Ethan keep his job.

He went to Josh's office to say hello.

"Hey man how are you doing?" asked Ethan.

"Great, how about you?"

"Okay. I am overloaded with paperwork."

"Yeah same here. They are really piling it on us."

"I know. It's insane. Well I just wanted to stop by. I will talk to you tomorrow, I'm heading home."

"Oh alright, I will talk to you then!"

Ethan got in his Ford Fusion. To save their company money, they switched from the Ford Taurus, to the Fusion, which isn't a bad car after all. He took it out of park and drove to their local toy store, and got his little Juliette a doll for her birthday. He drove home, and when he finally opened the door a little girl came running up to him as she always did when he got home from work.

"Daddy!" said Juliette.

"Hey Pumpkin!" She ran to give Ethan a hug, and when she did he heard a loud thump. She was just about the height that when she gave him a hug, her head hit the metal on his belt.

"Hi, honey," he said to his wife Ruth and gave her a kiss.

Nobody Wins

2

ETHAN WALKED DOWN THE LONG WARM HALLWAY of his home to answer the door. There stood a very old man. The man's jacket consisted of many holes, and it looked as if a piece of rusty metal hung limp around his upper body. His eyes were browner then Ethan had ever seen. His back was bent. Ethan realized this man had to be homeless.

The man looked very sick.

"Can... I use your phone sir?" asked the old man. Ethan, being the good man he was, was alright with it.

"Sure you can." said Ethan.

Ethan sat there while the old man turned around. Ethan couldn't hear what the person on the other line was saying, but he could hear yelling.

"Yes. Of course, I got it," said the old man talking on the phone.

What homeless man would need to borrow a cell phone? Who would he need to call?

Click.

The old man gave the phone back to Ethan.

"Thank you very much kind sir."

Ethan smiled,

"You're welcome."

Ethan walked into his living room, where his beautiful daughter Juliette sat. His wife was in the kitchen. Ethan looked at Juliette, then Ruth.

"Who was that honey?" asked Ruth.

"I think it was a homeless man; he asked to use my phone."

"You got your phone back, right?"

"Yes I did,"

Ethan walked over to Juliette.

"Now… what would my princess like to do?"

Ethan's daughter Juliette loved to play board games; it was her favorite thing to do.

Ethan had a very close relationship with his parents, who lived in Chicago, although he didn't get up there from St. Louis very often. It was as if Ethan's parents favored him, which in fact, they had. Too much. He had once had a brother who was named Cale. That name meant "uncertain". When the boys were young, you could almost say that they ignored Cale and only gave attention to Ethan. Why? Well, Ethan *was* the more attractive one, the smarter one, the first born, and Cale thought that he could never live up to his parents expectations.

One day, when Cale was 13 years old, he was out in the back yard and they heard a scream. Their parents ran outside and then the tree fort that Cale had been playing in had caught on fire. The fort had fallen to the ground, and they knew there was no chance he was alive. They found the remnants of the 13 year old boy's body. This changed Ethan's life.

His parents had learned through their grief. Ever since Cale passed away, they deeply regretted not treating him better. Ethan didn't know if he could ever recover from such a loss. He wished Cale was more loved; he didn't know how to treat his emotions. This was *one* of the reasons he and religion didn't mix. He had known about God, but didn't want to put his life in a God's hands that lets bad things happen. Ethan hadn't seen the big picture.

3

ETHAN WOKE UP AFTER A LONG NIGHT OF LITTLE SLEEP. He had been having problems sleeping for some time. He wished he could just sleep soundly through the night. Ethan looked next to him and noticed Ruth was gone; probably to work.

He thumped down the stairs to see his daughter playing.

He looked out the shades of the window and noticed it was a rainy day. He turned on the Weather Channel.

"The forecast for this week looks like its going to be mostly rainy with a high of 52 degrees." His favorite weather was dry and mild; this was his *least* favorite weather.

Ethan was a hard worker. He was President of Retail Sales at Comp City. His wife was the manager at a jewelry store. Ethan's job was to manage the sales people in the business, and make presentations. Although he did not enjoy giving presentations, that was his job, and he was content. He called up the babysitter about half an hour later.

"Hello Jenny? It's Mr. Monroe"

"Hello Mr. Monroe! Do you want me to come babysit Juliette again?"

"That would be great, thanks. I will pay you when I get home."

Ethan left for work.

He put the Fusion in park, grabbed his shiny leather briefcase and headed for the building. Ethan was very organized.

Currently Ethan was having some troubles at work. Profits had dropped rapidly, and he was in charge of making sure the "money charts" did not continue to drop any further, and at the moment, the profits were still dropping. It was very nice to have a wife that worked. Just in case something happened at his job, it offered valuable security to their family.

Bill Rockner was Ethan's boss. He was a small man with an abnormally large head, and if you ever entered his office you would see the top of his grey head buried in a newspaper.

Ethan looked around the room. In the corner was a leather couch, and there was a bookshelf with at least 300 books on it. Ethan directed his attention to the nice glass bottle of scotch sitting on Bill's desk. It was now 12:32

p.m. and Ethan's stomach started to growl. He got up and walked over to the vending machines. All that was in them were foods high in sugar. *That wouldn't work.*

He walked back into his office, filled out a few papers, and then noticed that his in box was empty. He could leave early.

The next morning when Ethan went to his work, he rang up the Vice President of Retail Sales. It was Joshua. He was a tall man with light blond hair and bright blue eyes. There was something about Josh that was different though; maybe the way he acted. Ethan told Joshua all about how the old man had paid him a visit.

"Wow, that's odd,"

"Yeah," Ethan said, still bothered.

"I mean, that could have been dangerous!"

"That's true. I am just glad my family is safe."

"Yeah, I bet."

The rest of the day contained more meetings and presentations. Ethan needed a break; he needed to get home. Finally he took off his suit, and changed into some jeans and a light weight t-shirt in the back room, got into his car and drove home. He came home to a group of people with eye to eye smiles on their faces.

"What's all this about?" asked Ethan
Then everybody screamed in unison,

"Happy Birthday!"

"What?"

Then Ruth responded with her eyes shining,

"It's your birthday honey!"

"Oh, yeah I guess I forgot. Thanks you guys, it means so much to me!"

That night, Ethan realized more then ever that his family meant everything to him. His family was his life.

Nobody Wins

4

ETHAN AWOKE TO THE CLAPPING AND POUNDING OF A THUNDERSTORM. He looked to his right and saw his wife sound asleep. He loved her so much. After about twenty minutes of tossing and turning, Ethan eventually decided to get a midnight snack. More like a three o' clock in the morning snack. He was sitting on a stool in the kitchen when the lightning struck again, and again. The thunder did not stop. The lightning struck again. Ethan was looking at the floor, but when it had struck he saw a shadow. The shadow of a man. He quickly looked up but didn't see anything. Was it that Ethan was just really sleepy, or were his eyes playing tricks on him? He didn't know until lightning had struck one more time. He immediately realized that he was not crazy after all, he saw the man running away from his house!

Ethan bolted out the back door and took off after the stranger. Ethan was gaining on him, or so he thought. The man was becoming less and less visible. The rain was picking up. Ethan kept on running after him as fast as he could, but it wasn't fast enough. Ethan had a feeling this was the man that had paid him and his family a visit earlier.

Eventually Ethan lost sight of where that man had run, but knew the direction. When he got home he called 911 as fast as his fingers could dial.

"St. Louis Police department, what's your emergency?"
Ethan began talking in long run-on sentences.

"I just saw a man outside my house…
and he ran away… and I tried to run after
him…"
Ethan took a breath.

"Which direction did he go?"

"He went south from my house."

"We will send two police officers over
there immediately."

"Thank you," Ethan replied in a shaky
voice, trying to catch his breath.

He didn't know whether to wake his
family up and frighten them by letting them
know there was someone outside, or just wait
until the police came and let them sort it all out.
He decided to wait until they came. He heard
the knock on the door. The police were there.

"Hello, I am so glad you're here!"
Ethan then repeated what happened, except
this time more controlled.
Then the officers gave him shocking news that
confused him.

"We saw footsteps running south west just as
you had described.   We will know more

when we find him. We will be on the lookout and will let you know as soon as we do."

"Thanks Officers."

"We'll be in touch."

5

THE NEXT DAY ETHAN EXPERIENCED ANOTHER PROBLEM that was quite a shock.

"It looks like it's official. We have no choice but to declare bankruptcy." said Mr. Rockner.

"What!? How can that be?"
He knew the company had been in trouble, but he thought they had more time.

"Well you knew the financial condition we have been in. The shareholders are closing in. We have no choice. "

"Does this mean I am going to lose my job?"

"We don't know yet," said Rockner whose large head had grown increasingly red.

"We are going to meet with the stockholders and should hear from the court as to what their plan is." From then on, the only thing that was good about that week was that he got to spend time with his family.

The benefit to Ethan's working at an electronics store is that he got a huge discount on all electronics. That day Ethan walked out of Circuit Central with a huge set of security cameras. Even with the bankruptcy over his head, family safety was first.

Better to be safe than sorry.

Soon the next day, he had all of the cameras set up, and the TV was set up as well. Ethan had been working on a plan to keep his family safe. Part of that was to find that old man as soon as possible so that he didn't have to worry about this whole situation.

He unlocked the door and entered in. Juliette ran to the door.

"Daddy!"

"Hey Princess!" Ethan picked her up in his arms and kissed her on the cheek.

"Where's mom?" asked Ethan,

"She said she would be gone for a little bit, but she will be back soon. Jenny is here with me now."

"Oh, I understand. Jenny?" Ethan reached into his pocket and grabbed a twenty dollar bill.

"Thanks, you can go home now."

A young teenage girl with a face full of freckles came down the stairs.

"Thank you Mr. Monroe!"

"Hmm... so Juliette, if you practice your violin maybe we could get some ice cream!"

"Really?"

Juliette was out of his arms and back to her room in a flash.

One of Ethan's love languages was most definitely quality time. He loved one-on-one time with his family.

●●●

An hour later they were at the ice cream shop. Ethan was staring into space worrying about how his job.

What if I lose my job? How will I tell my family?

He was reminded how grateful he was that his wife was the manager at the jewelry store, so at least they would still have some income in case something happened to his job. That night he finally came up with enough guts to tell his wife that Comp City might be going out of business.

"What?" asked his wife.

"I know. I didn't want to tell you."

"No, that's great! If it happens then I can spend more time with you, and you can spend more time with Juliette, I think it would be fantastic."

"Oh, really? Well if you think so, then I will think it's great too! I would just feel bad being Mr. Mom."

Ruth laughed.

"It would just be temporary though, until you found a new job."
She was always so calm when facing crisis.
"Yeah I guess so."

Nobody Wins

6

ETHAN WOKE UP JUST AS EVERY MORNING, still tired, his hair disheveled. He barely made it out of bed as a result of his lack of sleep. He arrived down the stairs and saw little Juliette playing a board game with the babysitter Jenny. He saw a blinking light on his phone.

He dialed the voicemail, and recognized Ruth's voice. She was whispering so fast he could hardly understand her, and he could tell she was crying.

"Ethan- come to the store. Please. Hurry! Help me."
Click.

Ethan ran for the door. "I'll be back Jenny!"

The drive to the store had never seemed so slow, even though he was speeding. He pulled up in the parking lot of the jewelry store, and immediately he noticed that the store blinds were closed.

He walked in the door and froze. There was a man holding Ruth by the neck with a gun to her head. The man had a mask on his face and Ethan couldn't see his features, but he noticed the man was fairly tall, very skinny. That's all he could see.

"What is this? I will give you anything you want just don't shoot!"

"Pack up the jewelry now." said the man in the mask.

"Don't do it!" said Ruth.

"Shut up!" the man screamed jerking Ruth's head back and forth with his tight grip on her neck.

"Of course I am going to do it; it's the only way we can get you out alive."

"Do it now!" screamed the man cocking the gun.

Ethan started packing up the jewelry as fast as he could. After what seemed like forever, it was finished.

BAM!

The sound crashed through the silence in the store. Ethan ran to Ruth screaming. His world fell apart right before his eyes. It was as though time had stopped. No movement, no heartbeat. She was dead. Everything that Ethan was was dead. The one who taught Juliette everything was dead. Ethan quickly sprinted towards that man, running at full speed and then jumping on the masked stranger. He made sure the gun was out of the man's possession and sat on his chest in the position to hit the man in the face. He punched, and punched. One punch came after another until Ethan lost control.

He had hit the man so much that the man's face looked like raw meat. Blood was dripping out of the man's nose, and poured out of his mouth. Adrenaline had taken over Ethan. Before Ethan could question the man as to *who he was* or *who he was working for,* the man pulled Ethan's leg. Ethan stumbled. The man jumped up and staggered regaining his balance. He looked left, then right and bolted for the door.

Ethan didn't know if he should follow the masked stranger or not. His heart told him to stay by Ruth's side.

Was this just an average person who was robbing a jewelry store? Or was this related to the old man? Ethan was sure that it had to tie together somehow, but didn't know how. Ethan ran back towards Ruth's body crying harder than ever. He bent down over her body, and realized that without her she had no reason to live. He reached his hand over her face and closed her beautiful eyes. She had changed over the years since they first met, but her eyes never did. The first time they met, it was like seeing a diamond shining in the sunlight. He would never see those eyes again.

He called 911.

●●●

"St. Louis Police department. What's your emergency?"

"My wife just got shot!! Somebody help me! She is not breathing. I am pretty sure she is dead."

"Hold the line sir, we will send help immediately."

Ethan sat and waited for the police to come to the crime scene while on the phone with the dispatcher. His thoughts were racing. He thought of Ruth, then dropped the phone and ran towards his wife so that he could hold his sweet Ruth's limp body.

Ruth is dead! These words spun through Ethan's mind over and over. He could not believe or accept it.

He saw two police cars pull up, an undercover car and an ambulance. Three men and two women came out of the cars.

"Sir- are you injured? What happened here?"

Ethan's whole face was soaking wet from tears.

"I got a message and-"

"Do you have the message still on your phone?"

"Yes."

"Can we have it?"

"Yeah."

Ethan reached into his pocket to retrieve his phone and played it for the officers.

"Okay sir, please continue,"

"Well my wife said 'come to the store and come alone.' I thought it was strange, but I did as it said. I drove to the store to find a man with one hand around my wife's neck and a gun to her head. He ordered me to pick up the diamonds or else he would kill her. I would do anything for my wife and so I did it, and he shot her."

Although the police men and police women could barely hear what he was saying from all the sobbing, they made out most of it.

Panic had taken over Ethan's thoughts. *Juliette!* He had to decide whether to stay with Ruth's body, or go make sure Juliette was alright. He had absolutely no choice; he made the right decision.

"Can I go check on my daughter?" asked Ethan.

"Certainly, sir. We will contact you for more information."

Ethan ran out to his car and sped home as fast as he could to make sure Juliette and the babysitter were alright. He ran in the door,

"Juliette, are you here?"

"Yes Dad, just playing board games."

Ethan still sobbing harder than ever, told Juliette that their mother had passed away. Soon Juliette was crying too. Seeing Juliette sob that hard, made his heart melt. He made a promise that he would never let anything happen to her.

●●●

Ethan did not know what to do. His grief overtook him. He went to the closet, and in the box in the corner was a gun wrapped in an old undershirt. Ethan grabbed it for the first time in 10 years, and made sure it had ammo. It did. He tucked it in his pants and continued to pace around the house. Ethan didn't know what would make him get out of bed every morning; he didn't have a reason.

Ethan told Juliette and Jenny to stay put and got in his car then drove it to the mall. He had a device on his keychain, and it was perfect in a situation like this. Whenever the alarm went off in the house, (which meant there was an intruder) the light on his keychain would blink, and Ethan would know that someone had broken in. He hoped that it would never go off.

Ethan arrived at the mall just to find Mr. Rockner walking towards him. "I am sorry Ethan, but I have some bad news. I hate to have to tell you here, but we are going to have to let everyone go. Lay you all off." said Mr. Rockner with a very straight face. He did not know what had happened to Ethan. He had been unable to call anyone, or think straight since it happened.

"What? You can't just do that!" Thoughts raced through his head. How could he bear so much loss?

"I am sorry Ethan, but everyone is losing their jobs. The court didn't approve the plan- they are selling off everything. Why don't you go try Best Deals? I bet they would love a man with experience in the industry. Don't worry, you will be okay. You are a great worker with much experience."

By now Ethan was in tears again, but this time even harder. His life was falling apart and there was nothing he could do about it.

Why me? Why now? Why is this happening at all? These questions troubled him so much.

Nobody Wins

7

ETHAN AND JULIETTE WERE BOTH PREPARING TO GO TO RUTH'S FUNERAL. They were both deep in grief and shock. Ethan wanted to make sure that Juliette knew that he loved her. He also wanted to make sure that she knew everything would be okay. He didn't know that for sure, but he was going to try as hard as he could to make sure she stayed safe.

"Alright, Juliette, get in the car"

"Yes Dad," replied Juliette, with a frown. They were half way to the funeral when Ethan broke out into a hard sob.

"Daddy, everything will be okay," said Juliette. She was one of the strongest little girls Ethan had ever met in his life. She was also so full of life, even in a world of despair.

They finally arrived at the funeral parlor and walked into the room. Seeing Ruth's body one more time was the hardest thing for Ethan, besides watching her die. He missed her so much. During the funeral, many memories began flashing through his head; pictures of the three of them splashing each other with water while cleaning the dishes, or picking out their first dog. Each thing brought him to tears. Finally the priest had said "Now the husband will have a few words." Ethan got up from his seat with tear marks streaking down his face.

"I would like to say thank you all so much for coming here. It means so much to me and my daughter,"

Ethan then reached down and grabbed a crumpled up tissue and brought it out of his pocket.

"My wife Ruth was always there for all of us. She was the kindest person I have ever known. She supported any decision that my daughter, or I made. I remember the sparkle in her eyes when she said the words 'I do.' I will never forget that memory. She loved both of us, and we both loved her. She will always be in our hearts." Ethan then walked away from the podium quietly crying, using what used to be a crumpled tissue. After the funeral, Ethan and Juliette stood in front as people came and gave them their condolences.

"I am so sorry," said one of Ethan's college friends,

"Thank you for coming," said Ethan giving his friend a slight smile, although under that smile was a burdened face.

"Ethan, I am really sorry about the loss. I want you to know I will be praying for you." said Josh.

Although Ethan did not believe in "God," he respected that Josh believed and set high standards, and he appreciated that his friend cared for him so much.

"Thank you Josh, your prayers are needed."

The drive home was very difficult. The car was so full of sorrow, and hatred against the man who had caused Ruth's death. It was very tough on Ethan especially. He had never met a woman as perfect as Ruth was. Ethan started thinking about the whole service again, and then he got to thinking about what Josh had said.

"What if there was a God?" The thought ran through Ethan's head a few times, but then he pushed it away and reasoned to himself that it is absurd for there to be someone who created the earth in one day. It was ridiculous for there to be a God who loved everyone so much, that he gave his son to die for anyone, yet would let horrible things happen anyway. It just was not true. Ruth was dead. It was just a story. Or so that's what Ethan thought.

●●●

Comp City had gone out of business. It was devastating for all the people working there, who were now unemployed.

After a week, Josh and Ethan set out to find jobs. They looked at possibly working at many different retail companies, and really were hoping for a company that would need both of them. They were a great team, and had developed a strong bond.

Josh picked Ethan up in his Toyota Camry, and they spent the day pounding the pavement.

On the way to drop Ethan off at home, they listened to the song Amazing Grace on the radio. Ethan sat looking at the radio for quite some time, wondering what the lyrics really meant,

> *"Amazing grace,*
> *How sweet the sound.*
> *That saved a wretch like me."*

Finally Ethan spoke up. "Josh, what do these lyrics actually mean?"

Josh's face lit up at the opportunity to be able to try and reach out to Ethan.

"Well, a wretch is used in the song because we sin, and are separated from God by that sin. God's grace and mercy, means God had such a deep love for us that he 'saved a wretch like me/us' by sending his son to die on the cross for our sins. That saved us."

"Wow. You really do believe in this, don't you?" Asked Ethan,

"Every word of it" Josh stated.

"So because this God has all of this love for us, he died on the cross for us?"

"Yes. He loves us with all of his heart." stated Josh.

"Hmm. But why? Why does he have all of this love, and why does he care, period?"

"Because God made us. He loves us. He made us to worship him, and to have a relationship with him. We couldn't have a relationship with him if we were sinful, so Jesus died on the cross and paid for our sins by doing that so we could have a relationship with him and so we could worship him."

"That actually does make some sense, but I still find it quite a bit absurd to believe that someone that powerful loves people like us."

"Well, I know that is a lot to think about, and it is very hard to take it all in in one day. But someday it may be a little easier to grab hold of."

"That's just the thing Josh, I don't think I will ever 'grab hold' of the thought of God. I am still going to think of it just as religion. It is just a bunny trail that people have followed their whole lives to make themselves feel better. Just because they had a horrible life doesn't mean there is going to be a better life after death. It's just going to be death. Not anything; we will be gone." stated Ethan very strongly.

"Well, not everyone believes... It's up to you, and it is up to God."

There was a long moment of silence, and then Ethan said, "I guess. It's just hard to believe. If he was there, and powerful, he would have let Ruth live."

Ethan did respect that Josh believed in something so strongly, but Ethan didn't think that *that* was the particular religion to believe in. In fact, he didn't believe any religion was worth much.

They pulled up to Ethan's three-story home and put the car in park. "Thanks for the drive. Let's hope we will get another job together,"

"I am praying that we do!" Josh said.

Josh truly enjoyed his friendship with Ethan. Their friendship had really grown over the time they had spent together. Josh really liked Ethan. He did not believe in God, but he seemed to have his morals straight. He usually stayed away from bad language, and most definitely stayed away from many sins that people pull in. But Josh knew just doing good

could not save Ethan. Josh was hoping that he was making a difference in Ethan's life.
And what a difference he was making.

Nobody Wins

8

TWO WEEKS LATER THINGS HAD SETTLED MORE INTO A ROUTINE. The grief was subsiding some and now came in waves.

Ethan got an important phone call. It was a company calling, telling Ethan he had a job. The news made Ethan so happy that he immediately called Josh and told him the great news. Josh was just as happy, maybe even more than Ethan had been. Josh told him he had received an offer from that company as well!

A week later Josh and Ethan carpooled to work and started their new job, which included meeting their new boss. Ethan liked this boss way more then Mr. Rockner. His name was Jack Brown. Jack was a laid back, but very professional business man.

"Hello, you guys must be Ethan Monroe, and Josh Anderson."

"Yes we are" replied Ethan.

"We are pleased to have you guys work for us." said Jack giving them a smile.

"We are looking forward to working here," said Josh.

"That's the spirit! Let me show you guys to your offices."

Jack showed them to two different huge offices with brass name plates on front of their doors, and on their desks.

"These are amazing!" said Josh.

"Yes, they are quite nice. I hope you men put them to good use."

"We will" they both agreed.

Ethan sat down in his poofy leather recliner seat, and realized how lucky he was to have this great of a job with his best friend. It was the only decent thing that had happened since his wife's death. Ethan walked around the building and introduced himself to some of the fellow workers, met his secretary, and took a few calls. He realized that as traumatizing as his wife's death was, he needed to show his daughter how to be strong, and handle situations maturely, (although it seemed as if Juliette already had that handled).

Although Ethan had a new job, his mind was still being hit with one sad thought after another. It began with the thought of his wife being gone forever, and watching her face as she passed away.

Ethan's nice new wireless headset started ringing.

"Hello, Ethan Monroe speaking."

All Ethan could hear was heavy breathing.

"Hello?" Ethan said.

He heard a little girl in the background screaming. *That girl sounds like...*

Then it hit him. That was his daughter screaming!

Ethan threw down his wireless headset and immediately called Josh.

"Josh, I need to go home! I need you to help me!"

"Okay I will be right over!"

He gave no thought to the new job, or the new boss. He had no choice. He made a promise, and that promise was to make sure Juliette did not get hurt.

He did not know what was going on, but he knew he had to get to her NOW!

Ethan arrived at home and leapt out of the car. He ran into the house and saw Juliette and the babysitter sitting tied up in different corners of the room. They had rags tightly tied to their mouths, and were blind-folded. As he was untying them, he noticed streaks of tears down both girls' faces. Ethan had broken his promise. He finally got them all untied.

"I need to get home and tell my parents what happened." said Jenny sobbing.

"Of course, do you want me to walk you home?" stated Ethan

"It's fine Mr. Monroe. I just live three doors down." Jenny ran out of the door.

"What happened?"

Juliette trembled as she spoke. "Well, we were just playing a board game, and then I was grabbed from behind, then he blind-folded me. I couldn't see his face, but I know he had a very low scary voice."

"We need to call the police now." Ethan told Juliette. "Don't worry honey, this time we are going to catch them."

Ethan looked and noticed something on the counter. It was another note! Now Ethan was sure it was the same person who killed Ruth. He read it silently.

"If you don't want more of this insanity, you will do exactly as I say. -Vulture."

The note sent chills down Ethan's spine. He didn't read it out loud just in case it might frighten Juliette, but he did tell her how dangerous this man was, and that Juliette must never leave his sight.

The police finally came, took the details of the report, and Ethan mentioned that he had the security video.

He ran and got the security camera tape and together he and the police reviewed it. What they saw when they played it was shocking. They saw nothing. The whole video was just Juliette sitting in front of the TV. *This couldn't be the right tape! Was it full? No, it still had some empty space in it. And Jenny wasn't in the tape! This could not be the right one! Wait. Didn't Juliette say she was playing a board game with Jenny?*

9

ETHAN WAS SO TROUBLED AND CONFUSED. He didn't know what he did   to "offend" the guy in charge of this, but he was willing to do almost anything for it to stop. Ethan walked along the hall upstairs and peeked in little Juliette's room. There she was, sleeping. His little angel. He loved her so much. He then walked downstairs and the first thing he noticed was that it was incredibly dark outside to be 7:00 A.M. He turned on the TV.

All Ethan saw on TV was static, and what looked like a man. He flipped through all of their channels, but it was all the same. After a little while there was less static. Ethan wasn't able to make out a face. The face was wearing a mask. The only words Ethan could hear were,

"If you don't do exactly what I say…Hurt your daughter…"

Those were exactly the words Ethan did not want to hear. The next thing Ethan noticed after the static went away, was that the man had a low shaky voice. Just like the man Juliette described! He finally made out all that the man was saying.

"If you don't do exactly what I say, I will hurt your daughter in ways you would have never imagined. And you will watch it all. "

The video ran over, and over again. It was on a continuous loop. The man's low voice sent chills down Ethan's spine. He ran for his cell phone on the counter, slid it open, but there was no service. He tried to dial 911, but it didn't work. He tried the same with the home phone, but it was just one long continuous high-pitched sound. He ran over to the door as fast as he could, but it was locked! He finally knew why it was so dark outside; there were metal security flaps in front of the windows. Ethan couldn't get out no matter how hard he tried breaking through. Ethan's eyes started to water at the thought of something happening to Juliette. Fear welled up inside him. He ran up to her room and made sure she was ok as fast as he could. She was fine. He swooped her up in his arms and ran for the basement. By the time he had gotten to the basement he shut the door, and then locked it.

"What's wrong Daddy?" Ethan was breathing heavily.

"Just go to sleep honey, I will tell you when you wake up again."

"But I don't want to sleep."

"Just try."

Ethan was furious by now, and wanted to make sure that whoever was in charge of this suffered the rest of their life in jail. He plugged in the 20 inch TV in the basement, and heard the words over, and over again.

"If you don't do exactly what I say, I will hurt your daughter in ways you would have never imagined. And you will watch it all." Ethan started crying. *What is the point of life?*

Ethan was thinking about this for an hour. He had time, because he would not be going in to work that day. Ethan also started to think about God.

If there is a God, why would he let these things happen to Juliette and Ruth? These were some of the many reasons Ethan refused to believe in a supernatural creator in the first place. That's why he refused to believe in God.

His phone began to ring. Ethan gave a huge jump. The call had startled him. He looked at the caller I.D. and it read "Unknown caller" He picked up hesitantly.

"...Hello?" Ethan said

"Do you like my little show?" asked Vulture.

"Its you! You know what you have done to me? You know how you have ruined my life?"

"Yes, and I am pretty proud of it. Now listen up. Currently I have no 'errands' for you to run for me, so I am going to allow you to leave your home. If you talk to anyone about this at all, I swear I will kidnap your daughter, and I don't think you would like that."

"Errands? You're insane!"

"One more thing to add to your list of punishments. Don't say a word about this to the police. You know what will happen if you do. And don't even try to run away. I know where you are, and I know where you are going to be."

"Click"

He was gone. Ethan dropped the phone, and had no idea on what to do. He could not just live life as though nothing happened. He looked over at Juliette. Sweet Juliette. She didn't do anything to deserve this. He would take her place if he could.

Ethan immediately called the police.

"St. Louis police department, what's your emergency?"

By now Ethan had called the police so many times the police probably remembered his name

"Hello I just got a phone c-"

And his phone hung up. What happened? Ethan had to tell someone. Ethan got another phone call from the Vulture. Ethan hesitantly picked up the ringing phone.

"Hello?"

"Ethan, are you deaf?"

"Vulture?"

"Did I not just tell you not to tell anyone?"

"I…. I didn't."

"Oh shut up don't even act like I don't know, I know everything you do… you know what that means Ethan, you're not going to like this at all. And it will be on your conscience."
Click.

Ethan was choked up. *All I was trying to do was protect my little girl.*

Juliette was sleeping in the other room. Ethan thought he would give her another hour to sleep and then he would wake her up.

After an hour Juliette woke up. Something was wrong. Her leg was bleeding and she began screaming at the top of her lungs. There was a note tied around her neck.

"I told you not to tell anyone. Every time you call the police, the punishment will be worse."

Juliette had streams of tears running down her face and she was still bleeding. "Daddy, am I going to die?"

Ethan was holding her in his arms like a baby, (Juliette was very small, but not the size of a baby). By now Ethan was crying, regretting he had called the police. "N...no sweetie. What happened?"

"Some man ran in with something and hurt my leg"

"What did he look like?"

"I don't know Daddy, make the pain go away." Ethan held her tight, and wiped the tears from her face.

He immediately got the first aid kit and wrapped her leg with a bandage on top of Neosporin.

Up to this point Ethan had not really thought about food, and the fact that Juliette might be hungry eventually.

"Okay, I am going to pick you up now and carry you upstairs so we can get something to eat, okay?"

"Yes, Dad"

Ethan picked Juliette up and they both went upstairs and gathered together some food. He took enough for a day, maybe two.

10

THE METAL FLAPS ON THE WINDOWS all slid open, lighting up the whole house. Ethan and Juliette both blinked their eyes getting used to the light. Ethan walked over to the door, and turned the handle. The door opened.

Ethan finally decided that they could stay upstairs until they heard again from this "Vulture" person. *What kind of name was that anyway?* He was thinking of a place he could keep her where she would not be hurt any more. *A safe? No way, that's the stupidest thing I've ever thought of. What about plastic surgery? No, what are you thinking of Ethan? Pull yourself together!* Ethan was hitting his head with his palm. *Should I put her in a boarding school where this man couldn't find her in the group of children? It's a possibility, but if he found her it could endanger the rest of the kids as well.*

If Vulture is a man of his word, he said they could leave the house as long as they didn't say a word about the "errands." *Whatever that meant.* So it was probably safe to leave the house as long as Ethan could keep an eye on Juliette at all times, and they went somewhere crowded...

Weeks passed and he had heard nothing from Vulture. But the scar from what Vulture did remained in Ethan's memory, like a blood-thirsty tick attached to an animal. *Maybe he is gone? Maybe he is not going to continue his harassment!*

"Let's see. Where would you like to go for fun ...and I mean anywhere?" asked Ethan.

He was anxious to get away from town and think. He felt like a prisoner in his own house. A getaway sounded like just what they needed.

"A theme park!" exclaimed Juliette. It had been a few weeks since Juliette's leg was injured, and Ethan thought it would be fine to let her walk on it now.

Ethan and Juliette had already had a tough few months. Ethan wanted to be able to drown out some of the things that have happened over those past few months by doing something that they have never done before. An amusement park!

Ethan booked two tickets to Orlando Florida.

"Honey, in two weeks we will be able to go to the amusement park!"

"Really? Oh thank you, Daddy, thank you!" Juliette then broke out into some kind of dance.

"Ethan smiled; a real smile like he had not done since Juliette's birthday. Then they both walked downstairs, and had a lunch that tasted more delicious than it had for a long time.

The sleepless nights continued for Ethan. He was consumed with his desire to make sure Juliette was safe. He let her sleep on a little cot in his room for the rest of the week until they went to Orlando.

The next week they arrived in Orlando Florida and got in a cab to go to their hotel.

Juliette was beaming with excitement. She had never been to an amusement park before. This trip had almost made Ethan forget about Vulture, but not completely. Every now and then he could hear Vulture in his head saying "If you don't do exactly what I say, I will hurt your daughter in ways you would have never imagined. And you will watch it all."

Ethan could never allow Juliette to be hurt, but he wanted to focus on her having the time of her life, letting her have the memory almost every kid wishes they could have. They spent three days in Florida. The day they arrived home Ethan put his keys into the lock and turned the handle. He came into a room that was clean as whistle, except one disturbing thing.

In the middle of the room stood a rusty metal chair Ethan had never seen before. Sitting in the chair sat a type of dummy with hair, clothes, and a face. It was a life-size doll, except there was one thing about it. It was torn and bleeding. Its wrists were chained to the handles, and legs were tied to the two front legs of the chair. He made little Juliette who was smiling until now look away. Written on the doll's body was "Don't tell a living soul." The writing looked like blood. Ethan immediately tightened up again and realized his life would never be the same.

Nobody Wins

11

HAIDEN WAS WORKING AT HIS DESK as he always did. He enjoyed what he did for a living. After a few hours of work he heard a sound that concerned him. The window had blown open, and the sound of birds chirping snuck into his dead-silent room. He ground his teeth noticing that sunlight had gotten into the room along with the horrible sound of those chirping birds. He quickly limped off of his chair to close the window and the curtain, and enjoyed the dark, silent room again. Dark to Haiden was comforting, soothing and secret. It made him feel powerful. Sounds bothered Haiden. They interrupted his thoughts, and disturbed his planning.

He got in the scalding hot shower as he always did when he was stressed. As his eyes glanced across the black moldy wall, he noticed a new crack. After the burning hot shower, the rest of his day included much work, planning, and determination.

●●●

Ethan called Josh breathing very fast. He was stroking Juliette's hair.

"Hello?"

"Hey Josh, it's Ethan."

"Hey, is something wrong? You sound troubled."

"Well, Juliette and I just got back from the amusement park to find a bloody dummy tied to a chair. So yes, something is very wrong!"

"What? Do you guys want to stay at my place?"

"No, I don't want to endanger you at all,"

"I insist. Come over guys, it's probably safer here than there!"

Ethan looked down at Juliette as she looked up at him. She nodded her head, her eyes pleading. She wanted to be somewhere safe.

"Okay if you insist, thank you so much Josh. It means so much to us."

"Any time! Anything I can do to help"

"We will be right over."

The whole time that conversation was taking place, Ethan sounded very troubled. Josh offered up a quick prayer, and prepared a room for his two guests. About 20 minutes later, Ethan and Juliette were standing on Josh's doorstep with two suitcases.

"Hey guys come on in" urged Josh.

"Thank you so much for letting us stay." Ethan leaned in to Josh "Juliette is really taking this hard."

"I bet! I would have been just as terrified." said Josh.

"Thanks again." said Ethan.

"No need to thank me! How long do you think you guys are going to stay?"

"I haven't really given it much thought yet."

"You are welcome to stay as long as you need. It's not the biggest place, or cleanest for that matter, but you are welcome. Ethan, why haven't you called the police yet? "

"Well, he told us that if we told a living soul there would be serious consequences."

"Like....?"

"I am not sure. This man or 'Vulture' has killed my wife. Therefore I am not going to question it. Even though I think that sometimes, I wish there was a way I could put an end to him."

"Wait, what do you mean by 'Vulture'?"

"Oh, that's what he calls himself. I am not sure why yet, but I am sure I will find out."

There was a moment of silence.

"Daddy, what can I have for dinner?" asked little Juliette. Ethan chuckled.

"Sorry Josh, is there just something that she could munch on?"

"Umm, yeah let me go look."

Josh looked at her and gave a smile and a wink. They heard about 3 minutes of rattling pots, pans, and other noises that Ethan wasn't even sure he'd heard before. Josh finally came out with his arms full of food.

"I got some bread, some peanut butter, some candy, and chips."

"Thanks Josh. We'll fix up some sandwiches."

"No problem."

Nobody Wins

12

HAIDEN HAD A HOUSE UNLIKE OTHERS; it was a small shack next to the dump. Haiden had a right hand man named John. Haiden could always trust John to help him out with any work, or problems he encountered.

The sun came up as it always did, except this time when it rose, Ethan was still asleep. He slept in until it was 12:00 P.M. He walked downstairs and this time saw Juliette playing with a puzzle, and Josh watching the Denver Football game. He was tired of feeling like a prisoner, waiting for something or someone.

"Hey Ethan, do you want anything? I've got orange juice, coffee, milk,"

"No, I'm fine. Thanks." Ethan smiled for the first time since Orlando.

Ethan looked at Juliette.

"What do you want to do today?"

"Daddy, will the person scare us again?" She looked up at him with a helpless look.

"I don't think so honey."

"Then can we go get pretzels?"

Ethan laughed.

"All you want to do for the whole day is eat pretzels?"

"No, um… I think take a walk!"

"Sounds great to me" said Ethan.

"Do you want to join us Josh?"

"Yeah, that sounds like fun!"

"It's settled. Maybe that will take our minds off of this madness."

The next couple of days were perfectly normal. Three days later the Monroe's thought it would be best to move back in to their home. Josh drove them back to their house.

"Thanks so much again Josh; you don't know how great that was to get out," said Ethan.

"Any time, that's what friends are for. Any time you need a place to stay again, keep in mind I am here."

"Alright sounds great. Thanks again."

Ethan got out and helped Juliette out of the car. They walked up the front steps and opened up the door. When they walked up everything seemed to be normal. He searched the whole house. The coast was clear. Everything seemed normal except for the security camera TV's. You could still hear Vulture's voice repeating the message louder now. Ethan tried turning off the TV. It wouldn't turn off. He tried lowering the volume and it turned down. Then Ethan heard another message coming from the Vulture. Just like the first message, he couldn't make out the words at first.

"I want you to…from a store….if you want fingers…want your daughter."

Ethan's heart rate rose ten times. He stared at the TV monitor for a minute just staring at Vulture and noticed that the strange contraption on his face was a mask with a beak taped on. *This man is crazy*. He stayed in front of the screen and concentrated until he could hear the message clearly.

He finally did and the words he made out were, "For your first errand, I want you to steal something of value from the store, leave it on your porch at night, then walk back inside and stay inside until morning. I would suggest you do this if you want fingers, and if you want your daughter. You have five days."

Ethan was so mad he felt like taking a knife to Vulture right then. *Steal something valuable from a store? What's that all about?*

I would give up my fingers for Juliette. Ethan said quietly. But truthfully, getting his fingers cut off was one of his greatest fears. He was willing to steal something valuable from a store in place of cutting off his fingers, or having something happen to his daughter. A million thoughts ran through Ethan's head. *How am I supposed to just waltz in and steal something valuable? Why do I have to do this?*

Ethan wondered why Vulture didn't want anything in particular, but yet he wanted just something valuable. *It must be a test.* He wished he didn't have to think about it. But he did. That night he was up until 4:57AM trying to think of what to steal and how to steal it. Ethan knew that this man could clearly make his way in, and out of his house. He could tell by the bloody dummy sitting in the family room tied to a metal chair. When he went to sleep, he drifted in and out fitfully.

Nobody Wins

13

ETHAN WOKE UP ON A HARD SURFACE shivering from the cold. It took him a few minutes to wake up. He looked around but couldn't see anything. He got up and started to feel around, but couldn't feel anything. He heard whispers, but couldn't tell where they were coming from. Ethan suddenly panicked. He remembered that he was supposed to steal something valuable from the store or else he would either get his fingers cut off, or Juliette would die. But how could he steal something valuable from a dark wet place that he can't get out of? Ethan's eyes started to adjust to the dark, but all he could see was rough walls.

Ethan started to scream. He screamed as loud as he could. He felt sharp pain run up his hand. He screamed again, but this time from agony. He looked down to see bleeding stumps. His fingers were cut off. *How has it already been five days*? Vulture didn't even give him a chance! He could have done it! His hand hurt more then ever. Who cut off his fingers?

Ethan woke up breathing heavy, heart pounding. He checked his hands, and they were perfectly fine. He looked around, and he was still in his large king size bed he had gone to sleep in that night. He plopped back in bed still breathing incredibly fast. He looked at the clock and it read 7:24 AM. That morning was the first morning Ethan was sure he was going to rob a store. He wouldn't let anything happen to Juliette or himself. He wasn't sure where yet, or what. But he was sure he was going to do it.

That next day was full of careful planning, and consideration. If Ethan got caught, and had to serve time in jail, he wouldn't be able to be there to protect Juliette, therefore he was very very careful the way he planned. He pulled up a picture of the security cameras around the store. He would have to disable them all. Even if he had a mask, he needed to be careful. Ethan knew that most gas stations usually have the emergency buttons under the counter that immediately calls 911. Ethan would have to sneak around the back entrance and walk to the cashier from the side, then quickly make sure the cashier doesn't press the button, demand the money, then run off. He would have to make sure he had a transportation source to get away. A cab would do. That would not look suspicious; many business men in St Louis used cabs. That would work. Ethan had the fleeting thought that he had become like the man that killed his wife. Tears came back to Ethan at the thought of Ruth, and hatred was in his eyes. But he did know that he wasn't going to kill anyone. Plus he was doing this to save Juliette. He wanted to kill the Vulture. He checked in the belt loop of his pants to make sure the gun was still snugly tucked in with the safety on. It was.

I hope the Vulture finds money valuable. He walked into the security room, and found little Juliette staring into the screen.

"Juliette, don't watch that, okay honey?" Ethan picked Juliette up and brought her out of the room.

"Why does he want to hurt us daddy?"

"He is a bad person,"

"Is he going to hurt us? I don't want him to."

"No sweetie, he won't hurt us."

Ethan had kept the "errand" to himself. He made sure not to tell her anything that could worry her.

The next morning, the babysitter arrived as usual, and Ethan got ready for work. He left just like every morning, but this time he waited in his office until 11 o'clock. Ethan was getting ready. Wearing all black clothes and a ski mask, he had a plan, and he was sure it was going to work. Time to go. Ethan arrived at the street by the store, and ran in the side door with a mask screaming, "Everyone down now!!"

What am I doing?

The customers screamed and dropped to the floor.

Ethan quickly looked around the corner. He had caught the cashier by surprise. He didn't press the button. Ethan shot all of the security cameras then looked at the cashier

"Open this cash register now and give me all of the money!" said Ethan.

The cashier opened the cash register and gave Ethan a bundle of money. Ethan peeked in and saw that the cashier was telling the truth, that was all of it. He quickly ran out of the store and about three blocks up slowed down, took off the shirt he was wearing over the sport jacket and took off his mask. He was now a business man wearing a suit. The money was in a briefcase. He signaled for a cab and started for home.

"Where to?" asked the cab driver.

"8374 East Hillside." replied Ethan.

He had done it. And successfully. Ethan hoped that this money would be considered valuable enough to Vulture. He arrived home, gave the taxi driver a tip, and walked up to the front door. He left the briefcase on the porch as Vulture had wanted, walked the babysitter to her car, went back inside and stayed inside for the rest of the night. Ethan crept up the stairs and checked on Juliette. She was still sleeping soundly next to her hippopotamus night light. Ethan walked into his room, took a shower, and then slept soundly through the night.

14

I WOKE UP AND I LOOKED AROUND the quiet house to see if someone was home. I was scared, and confused as to why I was alone. My babysitter wasn't in front of the TV watching silly shows as usual. Things have been so scary lately. I ate some food for breakfast and then did something "productive" as my Daddy would say while I waited for him to wake up. I looked at the time and saw it was 6:12. I didn't know it was so early and never thought to look in my Daddy's room. I walked up the stairs, and saw a lump on his bed. I went up to him and shook his shoulder lightly.

"Daddy, wake up Daddy."
I kept on trying to wake him up, but he was really sleeping deep. I decided to wait until he woke up. I walked downstairs, and couldn't get the thought of the recent horrible message out of my head.

"I would suggest you do this if you want fingers, or on the other hand if you want your daughter. You have five days." What does errand mean? My Daddy would do anything for me, and I am lucky to have a Daddy like him. I walked down to the security room, and noticed the message was different. It wasn't the one about my Daddy's fingers being cut off anymore...the message said other words now.

●●●

Ethan woke up and about 5 feet away from the bed saw a pair of big eyes staring straight into his. It was little Juliette.

"What are you doing up so early honey?"

"Daddy, it's eight o'clock in the morning. I was up early, and I couldn't sleep. There's a different message on the TV screen."

Ethan shot out of bed realizing that he did still have fingers, and Juliette was still there. The money must have worked! He got out of bed and ran to the security room; he was looking, and heard what the low-voice was saying.

"Congratulations! You actually did get something somewhat valuable. I didn't think you had it in you. I will inform you next when I have your next errand, my errand boy"

"What did you do Daddy?"

"It's nothing honey, don't worry about it." replied Ethan.

Ethan was getting quite annoyed by the whole message repeating. He had a new project. It was to insulate the security room so that no sound would get out. Ethan was ashamed of what he had done; But he was happy that he and Juliette were both okay.

The rest of the day was normal. It was summer, so Juliette had a few weeks of break from school. Even if school was on, he would keep Juliette out of school just as a safety precaution. They both enjoyed the time together greatly. It was a good thing they got the chance to relax. They would need it.

15

ETHAN WAS PLAYING A BOARD GAME with Juliette. He had so much on his mind that he was barely able to focus on the game. He had things on his mind, and the world on his shoulders.

How am I going to keep my little Juliette safe? Will I actually have to run more 'errands' for this Vulture person?

His thoughts even drifted places they never had before. *If Josh is so into this 'religion' thing, should I maybe look into it more? No. That's ridiculous, if there was such thing as a God, He wouldn't let these things happen. If this God was so loving, why would he let something like this happen?*

"Daddy... Daddy... Daddy it's your turn." Juliette was waving her hand right in front of Ethan's face.

"Oh I'm sorry honey, I was just thinking about some things. Where am I on the game board?"

"You're on the purple dragon daddy."

"Oh, okay,"

The phone rang.

"Hello?"

"Hey Ethan! It's Josh. My sister is in town, and I was wondering if you and Juliette wanted to hang out at my place. I have board games for Juliette if she wants."

"Hey Josh, Thank you! Yeah that would be great! Getting out of the house for a little while might be for the best.

"Alright sounds great! Come over anytime."

"Thanks! See you soon."

Click.

"Who was that daddy?" asked Juliette

"It was Josh. He invited us over to his house, so get ready to leave. Okay?"

"Yes Dad."

Ethan and Juliette headed out the door.

"Hey Ethan, This is my sister Mary. Mary, this is Ethan"

"Nice to meet you Mary,"

"Likewise," said Mary with a slight smile.

Ethan began getting to know Mary a little, and they all had a great time. Juliette put together a puzzle, while Josh, Mary, and Ethan talked. They did not talk about the problems Ethan was having.

Nobody Wins

16

AFTER MY LUNCH, I WALKED OVER to the family room to find my Daddy sleeping on the couch. He has been sleeping a lot. I think it is because of the scary man. I do not want to go look at the man's message. But I had to so my dad could be safe. I walked over to the TV room, and saw something. All of our TV's were gone! There was only one thing on the wall, and it was a huge TV that I had never seen before.

Besides the new TV there was a bunch of wires, and an empty desk. I ran to my daddy as fast as I could and I told him what had happened.

My dad quickly went over to the room, and tears were running down his cheeks. I didn't like seeing my dad cry. It was scary. I walked down the stairs holding his hand down every step. I knew that my holding his hand made him comfortable, and he needed the comfort. When we got to the stairs my daddy picked me up and held me tight against his chest. He was stroking my hair and I could tell he was scared. I knew my dad loved me so much.

●●●

Although he was still grieving the loss of Ruth, Ethan was so happy he still had Juliette with him. He tucked her in to her bed, kissed her on the forehead, and said goodnight. When he clicked off the light switch and was walking down the hall he heard a faint little sound. He stopped and heard the voice calling, "Daddy..."

He walked back to Juliette's room and opened the door.

"Is there anything wrong, Pumpkin?"

"I just wanted to say I love you Daddy."

Ethan paused and reflected on how much joy kids can bring into a life. He was feeling as though he could climb Mt. Everest. He went to sleep with a smile on his face.

●●●

I had trouble sleeping that night. It wasn't that my eyes couldn't shut, because I *was* tired. It was just that I kept on hearing noises. I didn't know what was making the noises but I knew that if it went on I would not sleep well until it stopped. It was a continuous ticking, it wouldn't stop. A thumping almost to a beat. After that I heard one loud thump and then the rest of the noises came to a sudden stop. I became worried, because I didn't know what could have made the noises stop. I heard one creak in the wood floor as if someone were taking a soft step. I sat up in bed. No matter what happened now my eyes would not shut. I got out of bed and walked over to my door. I called out my daddy's name, but he didn't call my name back. I called out his name a little louder, but all I heard was a grunt. I had a thought that made me want to scream. Was the thump I heard my daddy? I looked under the crack of the door, and saw a pair of shoes, but not shoes that I've seen before. I opened my mouth to scream for help but before I got the chance the door swung open, all I remember was it hit me hard enough to make me fall.

17

ETHAN ATTEMPTED TO LIFT HIMSELF up from the floor and failed once, but on the second try he got up and stood. He didn't know what to think. He didn't know if he was having a terrible nightmare. Suddenly the phone rang. It was his parents. He ignored the call and then fell on his bed and started crying. He could not stop. He picked up a bottle of whiskey and started to drink. Ethan was never the type of man to get drunk, but he was starting to think that there is a first time for everything. He ran for the only TV that Vulture left in the security room, and there was a new message. One that made Ethan wonder what point there was in living. The TV screen showed something unimaginable... a little girl with her cute little thin wrists clamped to a cold hard silver metal chair. It was Juliette. Her head was drooping. He ran to her room. The bed was empty! Ethan started screaming and hitting the TV screen wanting to break it, but knowing that if he did, he would have no way of knowing if Juliette was alive, or not. Ethan didn't know how he was still standing; his legs were about to collapse. There was no sight of Vulture on the screen, just a loop of his voice saying the same thing over and over.

"Remember Ethan, one little call to the police, and you won't have your sweet little Juliette anymore." He studied the picture on the screen, taking in every detail. Surely there had to be a clue.... Juliette sat cruelly tied to the big metal chair, sitting like a sack of potatoes. Ethan felt so helpless. He couldn't help but scream until he had no more breath in his lungs. His sweet Juliette had been kidnapped. The one who called him back in her room just to tell him she loved him ... the same sweet little girl who Ethan looked forward to seeing every day after work; the one that held his hand down the stairs to comfort him. Everything had been taken away from Ethan.

He couldn't even call the police. *What am I going to do?*

●●●

The whole day he sat in front of the TV staring intently at Juliette, waiting to hear from Vulture. Surely he would contact him! Did he have more demands? What did he want? Ethan missed the normal day to day things he had taken for granted... watching her playing board games, listening to her hum as she colored at the table...

Each time he heard the voice on the recording say, "Remember Ethan, one little call to the police, and you won't have your sweet little Juliette anymore," Ethan's rage increased.

The closer attention Ethan paid to the screen the more details he noticed about the room Juliette was in. Besides the chair, the whole room was cold metal. The ceiling, walls, floor, and the chair were all metal. It looked like a warehouse of some sort. It was definitely not a place for an innocent little girl. It was the same as being in jail, except for the fact she didn't do anything wrong, and she was unprotected. *Where is she?*

She didn't know what would happen. All she wanted was her Daddy. Ethan noticed on the screen the little girl's head lifted. She looked at her Daddy, because there was TV in the cold metal room where she could watch a screen shot of her dad. Ethan could hear anything she said, but she couldn't hear him; she could only see him.

Ethan heard a sweet little voice.

"Daddy? Daddy....."

A man walked in front of the screen with his back to the camera. Ethan couldn't see the man's front side. He placed a table to the side of the cold metal chair, and then left. This made Ethan sink deeper into despair. There was nothing he could do! Every four hours Juliette was given the option to use the restroom. The chair automatically un-clamped her, and she could go to the back room. *Where could she be?* The questions were gnawing at his sanity.

There was no place she could try to escape to, it was a sealed metal room. She had ten minutes to use the restroom, and once she was done, she had to immediately go back to the chair in the center of the room, put her hands on the rests, and the cold hard clamps would close tight around her wrists. Twice a day the Vulture would give her a cold metal plate with a small piece of bread, and a small cup of water. Ethan couldn't help but want to break down. He didn't know what was happening, and everything was just a blur. But he could see clearly enough to know that he had lost everything important to him, and he had lost his best friend.

Nobody Wins

18

ETHAN DID NOT SLEEP AT ALL THAT NIGHT. He sat in front of the television set and watched Juliette sit upright on her metal chair. *This is horrible; I would take her place in a heartbeat. If he offered I would take him up on that offer.* Ethan's thoughts raced while tears were streaming down his already wet face. It was now 8:55 A.M. and Ethan was forcing his eyes open to keep a watch on Juliette to make sure she stayed "safe". At about 10:39 Ethan saw something on the screen that kept him awake. He saw the man on the screen again, except only his back once more. He placed something on the table next to Juliette, and then walked off. Ethan was seeing a pattern. Every once in a while Vulture would add one more thing to the table. After a lot of squinting, Ethan realized that what the man put on the table was a box of some kind. It was a rectangle, and was flat. *What could it be?* Ethan went to bed that night wishing he had never been born. He was wishing he could have been the one instead of his brother to die. Then none of this would be happening. Since Juliette had been kidnapped, Ethan had blamed himself for everything. Ethan now even blamed himself for his brother's death.

●●●

I could have given him more attention and praise for the stuff he did. That's why he killed himself. His thoughts continued. *I could have brought a gun to the jewelry store, to protect my sweet Ruth. I should have protected my little Juliette that night by keeping an eye on her instead of letting her sleeps in her own room.*

Ethan's eyes were starting to grow heavier, and heavier. Suddenly he jolted awake! *If I fall asleep, he could kill Juliette.* That was Ethan's motivation to stay awake. Unfortunately, his motivation only worked for so long. His tired body gave in to exhaustion.

●●●

Ethan woke up on his couch downstairs. He quickly walked in to the security room to find a surprise, but not a good one. The Vulture put TV's up all around back in to the security room, but this time, each TV had a different view of Ethan's sweet Juliette. One had the view of the back of the metal chair, two views on different sides of her, one on top of her, and one in front where Ethan could see his daughter slumped in her chair. She sat there, with her head against the metal head rest, her eyes barely open, and she was motionless. Vulture gave her so little food and water, she didn't

113

have the energy to continue to struggle getting out.

Ethan recognized something different about her since he last saw her the night before; she had small microphones strapped all around her. There were about 4 microphones spaced out on each hand, and continuing up the arm. On each leg she had 5 microphones, again starting from the feet, and moving up to her waist. Whenever she moved an arm, leg, or her head, Ethan would hear it.

"What's this all about?" Ethan screamed to the TV.

Ethan watched the person move into view again, back to the camera again, laying one more thing down. A night club. It looked like a small black baseball bat.

"Take me instead! Don't take the girl! Please, I beg of you. Don't do anything to harm my little girl!" he said to the empty room. Ethan's weak legs finally gave in, and he fell down. He lay on the floor crying.

Don't take her, Take me instead. She's done nothing wrong. He felt dead.

What could he want? I did everything he asked!

Nobody Wins

19

ETHAN DID NOT LIKE THE FACT THAT Vulture was putting things on the table in front of Juliette. He was growing increasingly anxious.

Once again the man walked in view of the camera, and set something else on the table. Ethan's blood ran cold. A gun.

He couldn't shoot her could he? I've done nothing wrong! Ethan heard a new voice in the microphone.

"Do you want your daughter alive?" asked Vulture.

Ethan was screaming at the top of his lungs while clenching his fists, "Of course I do! I'll do anything!"

"Then do exactly as I say. You have exactly 24 hours to gather up supplies on the list I have given you. The list is on your front door."

Ethan was crying, but he didn't know if he was crying because there was a chance he could save his little girl, or because he didn't have her in his arms yet. Both. He ran to the front door as fast as he could. But he didn't believe his eyes when he saw what was on the list. The words seemed either be written in blood, or a smeared red ink. The list read:

- AK47,
-2 feet of electric wiring
-Ammunition for the AK47
-Ski mask
-Electric lock pick
-1 Taser

"You have 24 hours. If you aren't done with the list by then, go to the security room to say your last words to Juliette."

Ethan didn't know where the heck he would get any of those things. It was all too much, but he would stop at no costs to get Juliette back.

He spent 15 of the 24 hours looking for a place he could get the supplies. Once he had the supplies he plopped on his couch and sat there staring at the TV with Vulture on it. But there was something wrong; the 24 hour clock was still running down! It now said 3 hours and 46 sec. Ethan didn't know what to do to stop the clock. He remembered that when he robbed the store he left the money on the porch. He was guessing he should leave the stuff on the porch? But guessing wouldn't be enough! And he couldn't just leave a gun, ammunition, a taser, and an electric lock pick on his porch. They would have him thrown in jail. Although by now if Ethan didn't have the motivation to fight for Juliette he would almost prefer being thrown in jail.

It was late, and after waving the supplies in front of the camera for Vulture to see, Ethan decided to set his things on the porch. 3 hrs. and 23 sec. Ethan was staring into the monitor saying silently to himself, "Please spare my daughter, and take me instead." He finally found himself crying out, "Why do you need ME of all people to get the supplies? Why me in the first place? What have I done to ruin your life like you've ruined mine?" He wanted things to be back to normal, but the chances of that were too slim to count on.

20

ETHAN WOKE UP IN FRONT OF THE TV at the sight of his daughter sitting on the cold metal chair. He quickly looked at the clock timer on the TV. It was gone, and as far as Ethan could tell, his Juliette was still alive. He ran outside and saw that the things were gone, and the Vulture had received them. Ethan was so thankful that his Juliette was not hurt.

Ethan decided that if he wanted to save Juliette, he needed to be alive to do so. He walked slowly over to the pantry. He also decided he needed to change, and needed a shower. Once he had gotten changed and eaten, he walked back to the chair once again, and stared at his Juliette, thinking of a way to get her back.

Haiden jolted out of bed with sweat droplets across his face. He had had another dream; one of his dreams that made him think about where he stood in this world, what his accomplishments were.

The figure walked in front of Juliette's face again. Ethan still couldn't make out the person's face, but he did know it was obviously the Vulture. The man placed his hand on the box, and lifted the top of it off, then pulled something out of it. It seemed to be something that laid flat on the table. He pulled out one more thing... a pair of dice.

Is this man serious? He is going to play me in a game to see if my Juliette will live or die?

Ethan didn't know if that was what they were for, or not, but what else could it be? For Pete's sake they were dice! The man then walked out of the room. Ethan noticed Juliette seemed more exhausted than she had ever been before. Her eyes were bloodshot and her face was thinner. She focused her attention on the game board. Juliette loved board games.

●●●

My wrists are bleeding and they hurt a lot too. My legs are also bleeding. The strange man put a board game on the table next to me, but I don't think he knows that playing a board game won't cheer me up this time. I wish I was with my daddy. There is a big TV in front of me, and on it is my house. Almost all of the time my daddy is watching me, and he has crying marks on his face. I am glad he still cares about me, but I wish he didn't see me like this. I don't know what I can do to get out of this scary place. I just hope I can get out soon.

●●●

The TV that Ethan was watching so carefully suddenly went blank for five seconds, and then had a picture of a man with a bag on his face. He must have had a voice changer because it was ridiculously low.

"Do you see the game Ethan?"
Ethan swallowed hard.

"Yes."

"Is it not true that Juliette likes board games?"

"She does"

"Well then, I am sure she will like this one Ethan. Each space has a different crime on it. There are thirty seven spaces on the board, and one of them has an "Escape" option, and another has the "Capture the Vulture" option. If you land on one of those two spaces you get what they say. If you get to the finish you get your little girl back. They are normal dice, no trickery. Sound easy enough for you Ethan?"

"So you're telling me you won't hurt Juliette while we play this little game?"

"I didn't say that, did I, Ethan? There are a pile of cards in the center of the board. Each card has a different crime on it. If you fail to do the crimes on the spaces, then there will be a different punishment each time for your sweet little daughter; one that will make her scream, and also make you cry. Do we understand each other?"

By now Ethan was grinding his teeth.

"… I hate you."

"I asked if you understand."

There was a long silence.

"When does the game end?" Ethan asked.

"The game ends when you get to the finish. You want to get to the end…"

"Okay I understand I am ready"

"Good. Get a good night's sleep, you will need it."

Then the picture on the screen went back to the view of Juliette, and he could see again the view of her poor scrawny body that obviously had not been fed enough, and was showing the stress and anxiety.

Ethan didn't know what to do. He hated what he had done. He had only done it to keep his daughter safe. Anyone else would have certainly done the same if they loved their daughter as much as Ethan loved Juliette.

21

ETHAN WOKE UP AT FOUR IN THE MORNING. He felt sick to his stomach.

He walked over to the screen and saw Vulture with a bag over his face. Ethan looked at the screen and screamed to the empty room,

"Why do you wear a mask? What do you have to hide?"

"Ethan, Ethan, Ethan..." Vulture chuckled.

"You don't get it do you? Do you consider me a criminal Ethan?"

"I consider you a monster."

"Ethan, do you see a criminal, or a monster showing his face to the world?"

"I wish you would before you were sentenced to death."

Ethan knew he was crossing the line, but he needed to see how Vulture would respond if he expected to get out of this crazy maze.

"Too bad that won't happen, Ethan. Maybe in your dreams. The chance your hitting the space, is three percent. I will make sure that won't happen."

"But you can't make sure of that or else that would be against your word."

Ethan was grinding his teeth so much it was surprising he still had teeth left to grind.

"Time for the first round. Are you ready? Or do you think you would rather have me keep your daughter?"

"Is there the option of your death?" Ethan screamed.

"No that's not on the board. And remember, if you try to do something smart, or tell anyone about our little game, your little daughter will feel pain."

"You wouldn't" Ethan said with tears starting to stream down his face.

"Oh, I would. Wasn't I the one that stabbed your daughter while she was asleep? Yes, that *was* me."

"Let's start this sick game of yours."

By now Ethan had felt rage move through his body; he wanted nothing more than to get Juliette back, and to kill this man.

"This is what's going to happen. We are going to play the game in front of your sweet little daughter. She gets to see what crimes her innocent daddy is committing, and if her daddy is a good man and fails to commit the crimes, she will get hurt."

Ethan by now was thinking about pleading with the Vulture to stop, but he didn't want to give Vulture the satisfaction.

"Just roll the dice," Ethan said. He had almost forgotten what it felt like to see his healthy daughter in his home, safe and sound. The man rolled the dice out of his hands and they landed.

"Hmm… a one and a three, not so lucky for you." said the Vulture as he chuckled.

The camera was above Juliette's head and above the table so Ethan could see the game board. Little Juliette's face was twisted so that she could see what the game was. She had just learned to read, so unfortunately she could read what the spaces said. Tears were welling up in her eyes. She looked at her dad who was looking at her through the screen,

"Daddy, you're not going to do this, are you?"

Her voice was lost, and what was left of it was shaky.

"Sweetie, I have to," Vulture allowed Ethan to say to his daughter.

"Is that against the law dad?"

"Yes, But I have no choice."

"What… what will happen if you don't?" There was a silence, one that hurt Ethan's heart deeply. He didn't want to tell her that she would be the one to get hurt. Or worse.

"Nothing will happen Jules, nothing will happen."

Ethan lost it, he was crying again.

"Aw... this is sweet. Now shut up!" Vulture snapped.

"You rolled a one and a three. What crime was it?" Ethan asked.

"You landed on the space where you steal something from a man. But oh, what's this? Not just any man in particular... your father."

"What? You monster!"

"Now remember, if you don't follow through there will be consequences."

"What in the world am I supposed to steal?"

"Your father has a family heirloom. It has been passed down for centuries, you probably know about it. It is usually placed in a hole in the wall behind the picture in his room. If not there, then it will be in the in the wood box in his closet. Once you steal it, leave it in the birdhouse in your backyard. You have 30 hours. Remember; don't let anyone know about this."

If Vulture knows this well where a hidden heirloom is, he could have gotten it himself!

The camera switched back to Juliette's face straight on. She was tired, Ethan could see that. And she was afraid.

Ethan put his hands on his head and felt his hair between his fingers. He had never been under this kind of pressure before. On top of all of it, he didn't have his car back yet. He would need to take the bus, and he had to use cash, not his credit card. He would wait until dark, and then set out wearing black.

It was 9:03 and as he walked on his front step, he saw his electric lock pick, and his ski mask. That's why he had to get those things! For the game. It made sense now, but didn't make things any easier. He walked on to the bus and handed the bus driver several coins. As he walked to the back of the bus, he squeezed the ski mask in his pocket. He didn't want to do this. What happened to the man who had everything? A man who had a loving wife, a sweet daughter, and a great job? He lost them all. Everything except his daughter, although he might even lose her. And that's who he was stealing for.

The bus arrived to the intersection a few blocks from his old house. Tears came to Ethan's face as he was reminded of all the memories as a child; he loved his family so much. And his brother. His brother... The closer he got to his house, the more he remembered how it seemed that his brother was loved less then Ethan was. His parents weren't the best when it came to parenting, and Ethan wished his brother had been shown more love.

Ethan was approaching this place with so many good and bad memories; the place where he was going to commit a crime.

He looked out the back of their old house. His parents were watching the TV in the middle floor. *Easy enough.*

Ethan knew the layout; he knew where everything was. He reached for the door, it was unlocked. Ethan was relieved. He didn't know how to work an electric lock pick. He slipped the ski mask on his face, and snuck in.

Ethan knew just where the heirloom was, because it was going to be handed down to him. His dad had shown it to him many times.

It hurt Ethan so much to steal a piece of history from his family; something that meant so much to his father; something that had been in his family for so many generations.

He walked up the stairs as the old wood floor made a creaking noise.

Great. Just what I needed.

He made it into the room, and stopped pausing to realize that maybe... just maybe, he was one step closer to having Juliette in his arms.

He looked at the picture of a man looking out at a sea. Ethan knew that was the picture with the heirloom behind it. He put on some gloves so no one would see his finger prints, and lifted the large picture of the man and the sea. It seemed as if there was nothing there.

Did Dad move it? He wouldn't.

Right before Ethan put the picture back, he noticed something in the wall; a small string sticking out. He grabbed the string and pulled.

A compartment came out, and there was a cloth bag sitting in the box. There it was! A piece of family history that Ethan was stealing from his own father. Ethan grabbed the bag, slid the box back in the wall, and hung the picture up. It looked as if he had never been there.

Right as he was about to leave, he heard a noise. His father was coming up the stairs! Ethan looked to his left, then to his right. He had to hide, and quick! He leaped into his father's closet quietly, and crouched down in the corner under the hanging suits. As he looked out of the crack in the door, his father passed. He was walking into his room. Ethan was crossing his fingers that his father wouldn't for some reason check on the heirloom. Ethan saw one of his dad's slippers land on the floor, then the other one. The lights turned off, and Ethan knew his father was beginning to sleep.

"Great, a delay. I don't have the time for this!" Ethan said so quietly it couldn't possibly be heard.

Ethan heard something else. His father made a grunting noise. Then he started saying to himself "No, NO!" *It couldn't be possible! Did he check on the heirloom?* Ethan rubbed his temples. But right after that, he heard snoring. He checked around the corner slowly, and his father was sound asleep. He was talking in his sleep. Ethan gave a sigh of relief, and felt as though fifty pounds were taken off of his chest. He wiped his sweat coated forehead with his wrist, then he snuck around the corner and made sure he would not make the creaking noise with his feet. He saw his mom on the computer. He got past his mom, and was safely outside. Ethan took the ski mask off. He did it! He grabbed the bag out of his pocket and out came the shining jewel. What had he done? He had gotten closer to saving his Juliette. What a man will do for his daughter is unimaginable.

Ethan got in the bus. When Ethan got home he placed the heirloom in the birdhouse in the backyard. That night he slept soundly in front of the TV with Juliette on it. Ethan was glad he had gotten closer to getting back his Juliette, and he was hoping if he finished the game, Vulture would keep his word and give Juliette to him.

22

ETHAN OPENED HIS EYES TO JULIETTE in her chair. He jumped off of the couch and ran to the backyard then looked into the birdhouse. It was gone! It worked! Ethan gave a sigh of relief. When he walked inside he heard the phone ringing. He picked it up.

"Hello?"

"Son... our...the jewel was stolen from us!"

Nobody Wins

Ethan could hear how troubled his dad sounded. He felt terrible.

"What? How did that happen? Wasn't it hidden?"

"Ethan... This is terrible. That has been in my family for generations!"

His dad was crying; crying to Ethan about their jewel. Little did his dad know his own son stole it, or that his granddaughter's life depended on it.

"Dad, I'm really sorry to hear it, but I have to go. I hope you guys find it."

Ethan got off the phone and ran his hand through his hair.

How could I have done such a thing?

He looked on the screen, and he saw Vulture with the bag over his head just staring at Ethan.

"Aw, does your daddy miss his precious jewel?"

"I can't belie-"

"Yeah yeah I know I am a monster. I am surprised at you though. You did better than I thought. Are you ready to continue?"

"Let's get this over with."

138

"Here we go."

The camera switched to the overhead view.

Juliette's head had dropped.

"Juliette!" Ethan screamed her name. She didn't respond.

"Check if Juliette is okay!"

"She's fin-"

"I said check NOW!"

Ethan had lost it.

"She's fine. But she won't be if you forget who's in charge."

"Just roll"

He rolled the dice.

"A four and a two."

"What space is that?"

"Oh, not lucky for you! You have to kill a lady that works at the library. I want you to do this one fast. If you don't do it fast enough, she could call the police, that would count as a loss for you therefore Juliette would get hurt."

"What!? I can't murder anyone!"

"Well it looks like you've got no choice Ethan. After you do, take her wallet and any expensive jewelry she has. At least one

139

thousand dollars worth of jewelry and cash. I want it all inside the bin in your daughter's tree house."

"What? But I can't-"

Vulture grabbed the night stick on the table and held it over Juliette.

"I'm pretty sure you would want to."

Ethan had never killed anyone before! He was a good man, but did he have a choice?

"What girl at the library?"

"She's the only elderly woman there. She is about seventy years old and has red hair. She lives two blocks from the library."

"How do you live with yourself?"

"I look at it as an achievement."

"You're terrible."

"Did I mention you have 15 hours? You're wasting time."

Ethan jumped off the couch. The library was close, and because the lady lived two blocks away, Ethan could walk. He dressed in jeans and a plain shirt. It was not dark outside so he figured he wouldn't need black clothes. He waited a few hours. He still had time. He waited until four o'clock, when she was about

to get off of work. As he stepped outside of his house, he forgot his electric lock pick. He couldn't leave without it. He checked for the gun; it was still tucked in his pants. He ran inside and grabbed the lock pick; he then was on his way. He walked over to the library, and waited outside. He saw a few people coming out, and then he saw a lady around her seventies with red hair walk out. He couldn't actually commit murder could he? Would he?
I can't do this!

The lady got inside her car and started driving. When Ethan was a young teenager he was the fastest runner in his class.

Ethan started to walk but avoided making it seem like he was following her. He saw her house, but something unexpected happened. She pulled up to her house and entered. As Ethan approached the house she came back out.

Ethan leapt to the side into some bushes. *No! Ah she needs to stay inside!* Ethan had a thought. He wouldn't kill her! He doubted he could have anyways. He could just sneak in, steal what he needed, and then get out! He waited until she left and then got started. He went around to her back door and stuck the electric lock pick in the key hole. It worked. In a few seconds he was in the house. Ethan walked around and noticed that this lady did not have a bit of electronics in her house. She had lights and plumbing, but very little else. He walked up to her room looking for anything valuable.

Jackpot.

He found her jewelry box. It was way more than one thousand dollars worth. Maybe with that much jewelry Vulture wouldn't care that he hadn't killed the lady! He put the jewelry in his briefcase. It barely fit. Then he left as fast as possible. He got out and went home. He placed the jewelry in the bin inside Juliette's old tree house. When he got home he went to sleep again. He was not meant for this kind of thing.

23

ETHAN HEARD HIS NAME BEING CALLED. As he opened his eyes, the first thing he saw was Vulture.

"Ethan, you didn't do what you were told."

"What are you talking about?"

"You didn't kill her."

"Of course I did!"

"Ethan, don't lie to me. That will just cause more pain to Juliette."

"I thought since there was so much jewelry it would be okay if I didn't kill her. I was married to a woman that owned a jewelry store and you know that. I know quality jewelry when I see it."

"Oh, it's quality! But the space says you are to kill her first. I have no choice but to punish Juliette."

"Don't you dare lay a hand on her!"

"Be here to comfort her Ethan, talk her through the pain"

"Honey, Juliette?"

Sniff

"Ye-... yes daddy?"

"Everything will be okay you don't have to worry about a thing okay?"

Ethan's eyes were watering.

"Please don't, Please!"

Vulture picked up the night stick. He gave one hard swing and Juliette's arm absorbed the impact. She let out a scream, and Ethan heard something he never imagined. He heard the breaking of Juliette's bones. The microphones strapped to her arms and legs picked up the sound of her hand's bone shattering. There was a crunching noise.

She was screaming at the top of her lungs and crying harder than Ethan had ever seen.

Although Ethan was not for swearing, he wanted to now, more than ever. He was crying harder than he ever thought possible.

"I reduced this punishment because you did still bring the jewelry. I would recommend you following the rules next time."

Ethan didn't respond. He was in shock. How could he get his Juliette back? He wanted Vulture's blood on his hands.

The phone rang.

Ethan was still sobbing.

"What?" Ethan answered poorly.

Ethan? This is Josh. I haven't heard you're voice for a long time! Is everything okay?"

The sound of Josh's voice made him think of something; God. Ethan realized that he actually welcomed the thought.

"I… I'm not okay Josh. I need to see you. Coffee Café at one o'clock.

"Okay I will see you then."

Click.

Did he need someone to ask for help? Did he need God? He didn't think so, but he'd been wrong before.

He met with Josh at Coffee Café and spoke with him where the Vulture couldn't hear. Or where he *thought* the Vulture couldn't hear.

"Josh, there is a kidnapper after me. He stole Juliette, broke her hand, and is making me do these terrible crimes or else he will hurt Juliette."

"Whoa! Ethan, are you sure?"

"He has it all on camera on my TV."

"Do you mind if I pray with you?"

"No,"… he said quietly. "I don't mind."

Josh prayed for Ethan, and it made Ethan feel better in a way. It made Ethan feel as though he still had hope; like he was not alone.

"So this Vulture told you not to tell anyone, including the police?"

"Yeah,"

"Is that okay if I tell the police?"

"The problem is that I told you."

"But in a crowded café, He can't be everywhere," said Josh.

"The other day I found a mini microphone in my shirt Josh, I don't think he needs to be everywhere. "

"Well did he know you found the microphone?"

"I don't think so,"

"And did you take it off?"

"Not that day. I wanted him to think I didn't know" said Ethan.

"Good! And you made sure your current shirt didn't have a microphone?"

"Yes."

"Okay well I will call the police now." Josh said.

"St. Louis Police Department what's your emergency?"

"My friend's daughter has been kidnapped, and is being tortured."

"Where is your friend?"

"He is right here."

"Why isn't he talking on his own behalf?"

"The kidnapper warned him that if he told the police the kidnapper would hurt his daughter."

"What is the man's phone number, we will wire it."

"He isn't using the phone; the kidnapper put microphones in the house and can see him through his TV."

"We have you at the Coffee Café on Seventh and Main. Is that address correct?"

"Yes,"

"We will be right over there. Stay where you are."

They met up with the officer named Shelby.

"He tells you to do what?" asked Officer Shelby.

"Commit these crimes." Ethan said.

"Hmm. We've had no reports like this one for a long time. We most likely have not dealt with this man before."

"What can you do to help me get my daughter back? If I don't do the crimes on his little game board he will hurt or possibly kill my daughter! And I think he has my phone wired."

"Here Ethan. This is an untraceable pay-as-you-go-phone. Any time Vulture tells you to do a crime, go to a secure location and give us a call on that phone. Then let us know what's going on. Okay?"

"Okay."

She got up and left. Josh looked across the table to see a deeply troubled and lost man.

"Ethan. Remember, God is watching over you," Josh stated. "No matter how difficult things may seem, it's all in God's plan. And Ethan, just give praying a chance. It does help and God does listen."

"Okay thank you Josh."

They hugged each other. Ethan felt more comforted and was hoping that the police could figure out the Vulture's location. Ethan for the first time realized he couldn't handle this alone. He needed the help of God.

Nobody Wins

24

"ETHAN, WHERE WERE YOU?" ASKED the Vulture.

"I was getting something to eat,"
Ethan started to sweat.

"I didn't know where you were. I think the result of that should be punishment."

"No please! I promise, I wasn't doing anything wrong,"

"How can I know that's true Ethan? I can't, can I."

Ethan still had the receipt for what he got at Coffee Café.

"Look, here's proof!" He held up his receipt hoping that Vulture wouldn't see that it was for two people.

"I have to thank you Ethan, for committing all of those crimes and getting me this money. I'm enjoying this board game just as much as Juliette used to enjoy hers. Oh and by the way, you have 27 more spaces to go before you win Ethan. 27 more spaces."

Ethan didn't respond.

Vulture rolled the dice. Two sixes.

"Very well, you still have 11 more spaces Ethan."

"What am I supposed to do?"

"You have to light a building on fire. A building with people somehow locked inside."

"How the heck am I supposed to lock them inside?"

"Use your imagination, because if you don't, you know what will happen. You have 15 hours."

A crowded place.

Ethan changed clothes and went to the mall. He got out the pay-as-you-go phone and dialed the number the agent had given him.

"St. Louis-"

"Can I talk to Officer Shelby please?"

"Please hold," There was annoying elevator music playing in the background that made Ethan want to pull his hair out.

"Shelby here"

"Officer Shelby, it's Ethan. The man got in touch with me again. He told me to commit arson, with people somehow trapped inside a building."

"Did he give you any details as to how he wanted you to do it, how you were to trap them in a building?"

"I am not sure, but I need to find out what to do and fast."

Ethan arranged meeting up with Shelby.

"How does he know if you actually commit the crime or not?"

"He has me bring things back for him, and he had a mini microphone attached to me, so he can most definitely hear me and I think it's also a tracking device."

"Wait, what did you just say? He has a tracking device on you?"

"Yes?"

"Put it on me."

"What are you talking about?"

"We have to trick him"

"I don't understand. How?"

"I will put on your ski mask. If he is following us, then he will think I am you."

"You can hide and watch for him. If you see any car anywhere near where we are, you give me the signal and agents will follow him to where he is."

"What's the signal?"

"Here is a walkie talkie. Just click the red button and all it will do is make a beeping noise on my walkie talkie. "

"Okay, I think I got it."

"I will walk into a building with a gas can acting like I am going to light the building on fire, but it will be empty of course. I will walk in, drop the can so he can hear the can falling through the microphone, then walk out shaking my head as though I wasn't going to do it. When he realizes I am not going to do it he should drive home. But until he does, I am going to act like I am walking to your house."

"Okay. We have to hurry before our time is out! Where would we find a gas can to empty out?"

"We can stop by the gas station."

"Okay."

They hurried over, got the tank and went back to Ethan's home to grab the mini microphone. They drove up to a nice sized office building and decided it was perfect. They separated and Ethan stationed himself in the watching point. Wearing the ski mask, Shelby walked towards the building with the can in her hand. *Maybe the Vulture won't watch. Maybe he will only wait to hear the news reports about the building.* His hopes were becoming dampened. He didn't see any car. She was inside and dropped the barrel. As she walked out she started walking in the direction of Ethan's house. Suddenly something moved from Ethan's right. A man started running away! Was it the old man?

Ethan gave Shelby the signal. She ran for her car, hidden around the corner and got rid of the tracking device. As Ethan and Officer Shelby were following, the man took a turn to the road that led to the dump! Why would he base his hideout at a dump? As they got closer, the old man walked inside a small building next to a pile of trash.

"Yes!" Shelby said.

25

SHELBY WAS ON THE PHONE GETTING the S.W.A.T. team into their position. It took fifteen minutes for them to get down to where Shelby and Ethan were. They finally arrived.

"Alright I will go in first, then the S.W.A.T. team. Ethan, you can observe from here and follow once we have secured the building."

Ethan took his position. He watched as the officers slowly turned the handle then opened the door. They threw it open. Ethan knew they were close. Ethan quickly said a heartfelt prayer because he knew, just as Josh had said, that everything *is* in God's hands. He could see through the open door.

He saw Vulture! He was standing holding a gun up to Juliette.

It was almost as if time stopped for Ethan. He looked at his poor Juliette and wanted to grab her and hold her in his arms, but he couldn't just yet. He had a good view of the scene, and he could see Juliette. He had never seen her in such bad condition. The streaks down her face from a combination of sweat, tears, and dirt. She looked so skinny. He saw her injured hand and his heart sank. Her ankles and her wrists were both terribly bloody from the hard metal clamps. She had never seemed so helpless and weak to Ethan.

He couldn't help it, he ran inside behind the S.W.A.T. team. Juliette looked up and saw her dad, and once she did, Ethan saw her eyes filled with hope.

"Put down the gun!" Officer Shelby shouted and pointed the gun at the Vulture.

Suddenly Vulture turned toward Ethan and fired a shot hitting him in the stomach. The S.W.A.T. team lurched into action. They rushed around him with guns, handcuffing Vulture. Ethan found the strength to crawl over to Juliette, and rub his fingers against her rough, bloodied cheek. He mustered enough energy to speak to his daughter who he had longed to talk to.

"Honey, I love you so much, I am so sorry about all of this."

Juliette was tightly hugging her Dad who she loved. He had worried he would never see her again.

"Daddy, you're hurt!"

"I know sweetie, I will be better I promise."

Ethan was rushed to the emergency room. He was taken into surgery to have the bullet removed from his stomach. Vulture was read his rights, booked and was taken away by the officers.

Ethan began a walk of faith, and he became a stronger and stronger Christian. Josh had helped him through hard times and shared his faith with him, and Ethan encouraged Josh as well. Every Saturday morning the two men had Bible studies together.

Ethan visited Vulture in jail. He could see him behind the glass divider.

Vulture didn't talk but just stared into Ethan's eyes. Vulture went by the name Haiden. Ethan stared at this man who had tormented him and his daughter so much. He could not bring himself to pray for him although he knew God would want him to.

Ethan could not comprehend all that had happened these past weeks. He was more than happy to have his daughter back, and as beaten up as she looked, she looked more mature to him. She seemed as though she had grown in this time period of them being away. They spent a lot of time talking, hugging one another, enjoying each other's presence, and of course playing Juliette's favorite board games. Ethan listened to Juliette's story about her ordeal and tried his best to help her cope with the terrible memories.

● ● ●

When I saw my daddy's face, it was like a person's face when they see an orphan they are going to adopt for the first time. It was as though it had been years since we saw each other, and I had never been so happy to see my daddy in my whole life.

When I was at the scary man's place, he hit my hand so hard it broke. It still does not move but my dad said everything is going to be okay. And my daddy doesn't lie to me. When the scary things first started happening my daddy said everything would be okay, and it was hard for a long time but everything's okay now. My daddy did not lie.

● ● ●

Ethan left Juliette with Jenny and went down to the jail. He wanted to talk to Vulture

161

before he went to court, and was sent to another prison. He arrived to the jail and the first thing he saw was a desk uncomfortably close to the door. An officer sat in front of a computer as though he were in a trance,

"Excuse me,"

The officer looked up to see a man with a thick beard. Ethan had not even thought about shaving. All he wanted to do was spend time with Juliette. It took the officer a while to recognize the man.

"Ethan! What can I do for you?"

"I wondered if I could maybe try to get some information on this man, Haiden, or Vulture, or whoever he is. Do you know anything more about him? Have you learned his real identity?"

"No, we have no record of him. He had no identification. It is still under investigation. I know Officer Shelby wanted to talk to you and see if you could get anything from him. He seems to perk up when you are mentioned. She thought you might bring out something or be able to assist us in our questioning of him. I will have to talk to Officer Shelby first."

They spoke on the phone for a few minutes with Ethan patiently waiting across the desk.

"Alright she gave the O.K. Please follow me"

Ethan walked down a long hall. In the hall were a few locked gates, so if an inmate was to escape his cell, he would still be locked in.

Officer Shelby greeted him.

"Ethan, so good to see you. I'm glad you are recovering and that you've come. I'm hoping you can perhaps help us in our trying to learn more about him."

Ethan went through security, to make sure no weapons were carried in the jail. Then they came to the cell. Ethan noticed the man's face. It was very smooth. He looked surprisingly younger than Ethan remembered.

"What's your name?"

"I see you're still having difficulties walking. That's a shame."

"Tell me who you are. Tell me why you picked me; picked us."

"Let's bring him into the interrogation room," Officer Shelby said.

She and two other guards brought him out of his cell, and led him into the room. They sat him on a chair and then attached a lie detector on to his arms. After doing so Shelby walked behind the see-through wall so she watch.

"You know what this machine here does Vulture?" Ethan asked.

"It detects if I lie or not."

Ethan began to sweat.

"What's your name?"

"I never said I would tell you."

"Damn it Vulture! You were about to kill my daughter and ruin my life forever! So you better tell me your name right now!" Ethan said yelling and slamming his fist on the table.

"Ethan, can I see you for a moment?" said Officer Shelby.

They walked out of the room.

"Ethan, you are not the one interrogating him. You are just here to see if your presence helps him open up or give us some information.

Please try to control your emotions. He will get justice. Don't worry."

"Just give me a few minutes. Please Shelby just give me ten more minutes with the guy."

Although it was unconventional, Shelby sighed and nodded.

They walked back into the cell.

He looked at the man sitting there and began, "Why the heck would you choose me out of all people? Why would you almost ruin my life?"

"Cause you ruined mine. You really are stupid."

"What?"

"Does the name Cale ring a bell?"

Ethan's past flashed before his eyes. He looked closely at the man's eyes.

"What are you saying?? He died!"

"You thought he died."

"We found his bones! We had proof he died! This can't be."

"Did you really have proof Ethan? You really knew it was his bones? Or could it have been someone else's remains?"

"You're telling me that you are Cale? That you kidnapped someone and murdered him? I can't even begin to comprehend this! I still can't believe what you're telling me! How could I ever imagine I would see my brother again, and that he would ruin my life? I can't believe my brother is a murderer!"

"It wasn't hard. All I had to do was find a kid my height, tie him to the rail in the tree fort, burn it and run. I had all of my stuff packed before that. Mom and Dad treated me like gum under a shoe. They didn't care about me at all. *That's* why I chose you, you idiot."

So many tears were welling up in Ethan's eyes. It was like seeing how many drops of water can sit on the penny without the water spilling over the edge.

"You're not allowed to call them Mom and Dad." stated Ethan firmly. "You are a murderer. You are not my brother, and not their son."

"You are as stubborn as you are stupid Ethan. Look at the lie detector, I'm not lying."

Ethan fell down to the ground. He still could not believe it.

"Do you need proof Ethan? When you were eleven you fell down at the pool face first. Your right canine tooth is fake. That day there was blood all over your face."

"Stop!" Ethan cried out.

"When you were nine you tried fast food for the first time, and hated it."

"I said STOP IT!"

There was silence in the room. Ethan stood up and noticed there were no spikes of change in his pulse or heartbeat on the polygraph. He was running his hand through his hair.

"I know Mom and Dad were rough on you, but killing a kid your own age when you were thirteen to frame your running away? It couldn't have been that bad!"

"Ethan you don't have a clue. You have no idea what my life was like. Mom and Dad loved you; they adored you. They hated me. I'm surprised they fed me."

"They did not hate you. You were a messed up kid. They didn't understand you, but they did love you. And even if they didn't love you, that gave you no right to murder someone. Did you ever even talk to them about it?"

Ethan still couldn't even believe He was talking to his brother who had been "dead" for years and years.

"No I couldn't have talked to them, they never would have listened. If I could get out of here right now, I would shoot you again Ethan. You ruined my life. And I was so looking forward to ruining yours too. You had it all Ethan, you had it all."

"And you took it all Cale."

Ethan was silent. He was wondering if he even wanted to stay in that room and talk with Cale, or not. Cale was not his brother anymore; he was some filthy killer who had tried to ruin Ethan's life. He was a monster.

Ethan looked at Cale. "I'm sorry for you. Good bye, Cale."

Ethan walked out of that room. It was the last time he ever saw his brother again.

His phone started ringing.

"Ethan! It's Josh! Can we please meet?"

"Yeah, I'll see you at the deli restaurant in the mall."

"Okay."

They met at the mall and Ethan reported everything that happened. Josh sat in shock.

"Ethan, God's hand truly was over you guys protecting you all the way, I mean it seemed that the fact you saved Juliette right before Cale tried to kill her, couldn't just be coincidence."

"I can still barely comprehend all that has happened."

Ethan and Josh had developed such a close bond during their Bible studies. Ethan learned so much, and he really trusted Josh's advice and opinions and knew he could learn so much from him.

Ethan was loved by God. He was in His care. Even through the difficult times.

"Will you pray with me?"

"Of course I will."

That day meant a lot in Ethan's spiritual life. He followed God every day of his life from then on, and did it full heartedly. He taught Juliette what he had learned. 5 years later he traveled the globe sharing his story to churches around the world, seeing other people's lives changed as a result of the gospel as well as his own life.

One step at a time.

Epilogue:

TAPESTRY

"Book 2 of 2"

31 years later…

"If you don't do what I say there will be serious consequences."

Juliette, now 37 years old, was having a nightmare. It was like a memory from her past; more like a flashback actually. This one, she couldn't get out of. It was dream that she had almost every night, reliving the suffering, and reliving the pain.

Ethan Monroe was in the hospital with Amyotrophic Lateral Sclerosis, known as Lou Gehrig's disease. His muscles were becoming smaller, and weaker until eventually he would die. It was getting worse; his muscle function was decreasing rapidly.

Juliette didn't know what to do but to *pray*. Ruth's passing away changed Juliette's way of looking at life. It also gave her more of a pessimistic view of things at times, in spite of her faith. She struggled with this when she faced difficult times.

Juliette's hand was crippled from Cale's night stick landing harshly on her fragile hand. The impact on her bones was equivalent to glass shattering on the floor. The surgeries had helped some, but she never fully regained its use. *It's all in God's plan,* she reminded herself.

Juliette lived in New York City. Ever since she was a little girl, she had always loved the big city. She lived in an apartment not too far away from Central Park. Not a fancy one, but a modest one. She loved where she was, and also enjoyed her job very much.

Juliette was a social worker, and she tried to ensure that all the adopted children she worked with had loving homes; ones that were welcoming the kids with open arms.

She had an appointment today; a little boy named Jonathan Prickler. His parents were Jack and Madison. The boy was from Lithuania, and was 4 years of age. She had never met them before. They were a referral from another agency.

Juliette walked up to the Prickler's house and rang the doorbell.

A lady with heavy bags under her eyes answered the door.

"Hello, my name is Juliette Monroe. Is this the Prickler residence?"

Sniff

"Yeah."

"This is the residence of Jonathan, am I correct?"

"Mmhmm."

"Well, may I come in and see little Johnny?"

"Yeah sure."

Juliette already didn't like the mother, but she knew not to make snap judgments. She made a mental note and went on into the house. She still had some hopes for the father. As Juliette walked into the snug house, a large heavy-set man walked up to greet Juliette.

"Hello, my name is Jack. You must be Juliette." The heavy man said with a grin.

"Yes, I am she. Very nice to meet you Mr. Prickler. So where is Jonathan?"

"Well, you see, there's a problem."

Like I haven't heard that before in my career.

"Well, what seems to be the problem Mr. Prickler?"

"You can call me Jack,"

"Oh, I'm sorry. What seems to be the problem Jack?"

"Well, just the other day we took John to the park so he could play, but he fell off the monkey bars and face-planted into the cement."

"Oh no!"

She didn't buy it one bit. When parents adopt a child and have them for just over a month, usually the kids don't get injured in their face. It most likely would have been abuse, but of course, Juliette did not know for sure, and couldn't prove anything. *Yet.*

●●●

A lovely nurse walked into the room.

"Hello Mr. Monroe, Here is your daily medication."

"Thanks" Ethan said with a warm grin.

"Absolutely. Let me know if you need some pain relief."

The nurse brought in a small tray with a cup of water, and a small little cup with six different pills in it.

Ethan had lived a remarkable life and had an amazing story. He had gone to churches all around the world to share it with, but unfortunately that part of his journey had ended. His time here on earth was coming to an end, and he knew it. He didn't even want to continue on. He wanted to pass away quickly to be with the Lord. The pain was too great. Ethan hated to be such a burden to people around him.   Ethan was dying.

●●●

Juliette was almost positive that the parents were stalling. They kept on talking with Juliette.

"Oh well we warned you... he took a pretty hard fall."

"Yes, I have seen terrible things before, believe me. Where is Jonathan?"

Jack got up after some struggle getting off the couch. He then brought the boy down. He was the most adorable little boy she had ever seen. His little face was covered with bruises all over his head and the one cut on his forehead. He had big eyes and a tiny nose. Juliette watched him look up at her with inquisitive eyes.

"How did you say this happened?" asked Juliette.

"Well, he was on the monkey bars-"

"Yeah the monkey bars" mumbled the wife.

Jack looked at Madison and continued.

"... and then he fell and went face first into the cement."

"And just how did he go from arms in the air, feet pointing down, to face in the cement?"

Jack looked at Madison as if it was her turn to answer. She looked at the floor.

"Well, he is a clumsy boy." stated Madison.

"I would like to ask the boy a few questions. Don't worry they are easy ones so he can understand."

The couple hesitated, and then nodded.

Juliette got on her knees, "Johnny? Are your parents good to you? Are your parents nice to you?"

"Johnny looked up at his parents past Juliette's shoulder, and his eyes met hers again.

"Y...yes..."

"I want you to just look at me, not at your parents this time. Are your mommy and your daddy nice to you?"

"Yes."

"Do your parents feed you enough?"

"Yes."

"What has been your favorite thing to do?"

Jonathan's mouth gaped open but no words came out. He looked back up at his parents then looked back down.

"So...soccer"

"Did you get to play soccer?"

"Yes"

She knew there was more... she was not getting anywhere with the boy. He just did not have good enough command of the English language yet.

He seems scared to tell me something.

At times Juliette felt as though she were an undercover cop. This was the hard part of her job.

She got back up from being on her knees and sat back on the itchy plaid couch. As she sat down it smelled odd. The house most definitely had a distinct smell, not a good one. She looked at Johnny one more time, "How many times do you eat every day?"

Johnny looked down at his hands. He seemed happy that he could understand her, and he held up a hand with three fingers; he had counted to three.

"Okay," Juliette wrote some things on her note pad, then asked a few more questions of Jack, who wore a fake grin with his jaw slightly askew, and Madison who looked like she had no interest in it whatsoever.

●●●

Ethan could feel less and less control over his muscles; they were getting weaker and weaker.

Every few seconds he could hear the *beep* of his heart rate on the monitor. Eventually he didn't even notice it, except for when it skipped a beat.

This day, something was different. It started getting slower and slower, until eventually it was too slow, and then his world faded into black.

"Ethan Monroe's room! Stat!" screamed a nurse.

A doctor rushed in and quickly put electric pulse signals into Ethan's chest, desperately trying to revive him. After several tries, Ethan jolted awake.

Please God, Just let me die and be with you!

Two hours later he still had one nurse and doctor in his room with him. He picked up his Bible and began to read it again. What a comfort those words brought him. He propped open the Bible to Philippians 1:21. *For me to live is Christ, and to die is gain.* There was one part of that verse that Ethan was *trying* to grab hold of but was especially hard at this time.

For me to live is Christ.

Ethan had wanted to worship God in heaven so much, he hadn't been able to grasp what it meant when it said we are to live as Christ while we are *here*. God has not brought him to heaven yet, so he needed to live for Him here. He needed to accept God's timing for his life, and live out the days God gives him here.

Ethan let that thought sink in, while the doctor checked his pulse, heart rate, and checked his overall health. He would concentrate on that. For the days God gives him, he would serve Him; not think about his pain. *To live is Christ.*

●●●

Juliette had much to think about in the car ride home after the meeting with the Prickler's.

Could the bruises have been abuse? Or were they actually telling the truth? The questions kept running through her head like a loop. She kept thinking of them, trying to find the answer. She looked at her notes and forgot she had her cell phone on silent. She got it out of her brown leather purse and flipped it open.

The message light was on. Five new messages. It was the hospital. *Oh no!* She quickly hit the return call button. The nurse picked up.

"Good, Ms. Monroe, I'm glad you called back. You should come in to the hospital; your father had a stroke."

Juliette's world fell around her.

"Is he okay?" She was almost yelling the questions now, running one hand through her thick brown hair.

"Yes, he is doing fine now. But he would like to see you."

"Okay I will be over immediately!"

"I will tell him."

●●●

Johnny spent the night crying. Some of the lesions on his face had become infected.

"Shut up in there!" Jack screamed.

Johnny thought all people in America were monsters. He thought all people in America were like his parents. He got out of bed to get a glass of water. On his way back he tripped; it felt to him like slow motion. On his way down the metal hanger hooked into his cut and made his wound larger. He was bleeding more than he ever had before.

Madison came banging in the door with a vodka bottle in one hand.

"Why you be screamin' like that? You're hurtin' my ears!"

Johnny didn't even pay attention to what his mom was telling him because he was screaming too loud now.

"I'm tellin' you boy you better stop your screamin' or else you're going to get it!"

His screaming was still loud and growing louder. He was just a four year old; no four year old could endure that kind of intense pain.

"That's it little kid!" Johnny's mom screamed.

She took the wooden spoon sitting on his dresser and walked up to him swinging. Johnny's voice didn't alter because he was already yelling as loud as his vocal chords would allow.

●●●

Johnny woke up with bruises all over his body, and a towel strapped around his head. It was soaked in blood. As he got up, he took off the towel and saw a bloody wooden spoon sitting on a table by his head; the stick that his new mommy had hit him with. He was afraid to leave his room for fear of his parents beating him again. It was almost noon, and he knew he had to eventually get out of his room. He crept out of his room and found his dad asleep on the couch saying some nonsense. Johnny didn't wake him. Madison was gone somewhere; he didn't know where. He thought about the nice lady that had come to ask him questions. She was nice. He liked her.

●●●

Juliette arrived at the hospital, greeting her father with a huge kiss on the cheek, and a hug. She was so happy and relieved to see him.

"Juliette honey, I was out for a while. They revived me."

"Dad! Oh my gosh! Are you sure you are okay?"

"Yes, I am doing fine."

"Thank heavens they revived you!"

"That's just the thing honey, I am becoming older and older. Not to mention increasingly slow, and more of a burden to people around me-"

"Dad, you need to stop thinking of yourself as a burden."

"Well, either way I am becoming increasingly slow; I think we both know where this disease is leading me."

"No! Dad, don't think like that, I can't let you think like that!"

"But, sweetie, I don't think you understand. I want to be with God in heaven. This earth holds no appeal for me; it doesn't satisfy my desires."

"You can't leave me Dad! You are my father....the one who swooped in the door when your brother was about to kill me, the one that risked his life for me, you can't! You can't just... just die!"

"Okay shhhh it's okay. Forget I said anything."

"How can I forget you said it?" Tears were welling up in her eyes, like a dam holding back a lake. The dam was about to break releasing all of her tears across her soft cheeks. She looked at her father as if he had betrayed her.

How could you?

"Honey, you have always been strong, and I need you to be strong now. We can't be unreal about this. Everyone has to come to an end eventually. I think my end has just about come. God will be with you."

She looked at him, tears running down her cheeks, spilling out of her bright eyes. She shook her head.

She couldn't be strong, could she?

"Juliette, remember when you were the little one holding my hand to comfort me, during the time when my brother was playing games with us?"

Juliette sniffed a few times.

"Yes,"

"Well, I think it is the time I need to hold your hand, and possibly comfort you a little. You need to understand, I want to be in heaven!"

Does he understand I want him here to comfort me? To help me through many situations which I could not get through without him?

...I am selfish.

"I will try my hardest to understand."

"That's my strong girl," said Ethan while rubbing her head with his hand like when she was a little girl.

Oh the times we had together! Through thick and thin...

Juliette sat there and talked about life with her dad. She didn't get to do it that often, so she tried to make the time she had with him very special.

●●●

Juliette called Joshua Anderson up on the phone. He had always been a great friend to her dad. He was the one responsible for first sharing with Juliette and Ethan the truth about God. She asked to meet with him and pray with him for her father. He of course agreed.

Josh now had a beautiful wife, and two kids; a boy, and a girl. They invited Juliette over to dinner and she accepted with gratitude.

She arrived at their house and they opened the door.

"Juliette! Great to see you again,"

She kissed his cheek and hugged his wife, Hannah. As she walked in she saw a big weaving loom. She had never seen one before. Josh saw her staring at it.

"Do you know what that is?" asked Josh.

"No."

"Hannah has taken up making tapestries. This one is almost done!"

"Oh wow! Does it take long?"

"More than you know," Hannah said with a chuckle and a smile. Juliette really liked her and the two had become good friends.

Why would someone make a tapestry? It just looks like a bunch of random colors and knots. It doesn't look pretty at all...

Juliette of course did not say that to her friend, even though she did wonder a bit about Hannah's sense of taste.

They had a great dinner, and they prayed for her father. Josh and Ethan had been so close. After Juliette told Josh about Ethan wanting to pass away to go to heaven Josh was troubled.

Juliette thanked Josh and Hannah for their generosity, looked once more at the strange tapestry, and left their house.

●●●

Although Juliette knew she was helping little kids, and made sure the homes were suitable for them, she still felt like she hadn't done much in her life besides doing her job, and visit her dad. She knew God used her in the work with kids. That's why she went into that field. But she wanted more than that. She wanted somehow to do more with her life.

●●●

Johnny was awkwardly standing, staring at his intoxicated father while he was sleeping on the couch. His mom came stumbling into the room, eyes wide open, mouth agape. She was staring at Johnny with her blood-shot eyes.

"Who are you staring at? Huh?"

Johnny's eyes began to water. His dad got drunk a lot, but beat him less than his mom. His mom was the one who had beaten him constantly over the past month and a half.

Madison went over to the cabinet and grabbed a bottle of vodka. She slid on to the floor and sat there drinking. Johnny stood watching his drunk parents. If Johnny didn't get help soon, he would have a terrible future ahead of him.

●●●

Kaitlynn, age 9, was adopted by Adam and Carrie Brown. Juliette walked up to their modest country home. A nice couple answered the door.

"Hello, is this the Brown residence?"

"Yes it is. You must be Juliette."

"Yes. May I see Kaitlynn?"

"Of course. Come on in, we have iced tea and lemonade inside if you're thirsty,"

"Thank you!"

She walked in to a nice sized entry. To her right was a large staircase going up, and to her left were stairs going down to the lower level. Forward was the family room with nice couches around a TV on the wall. Sitting on one of those couches was a cute girl in a dress with long blond hair, and ocean blue eyes. Her parents brought out a tray with iced tea and lemonade.

"Please sit down"

"Thanks" said Juliette.

Juliette took a seat next to the beautiful little girl.

"Well, Kaitlynn, it's nice to meet you. How do you like it in America?"

"I... I like it very much" she said with a gleaming smile.

"Are you eating very much?"

"Yes, I have started calling myself fat," she said jokingly and put her hands over her mouth giggling.

She was a beautiful little girl. She had a bit of a speech impediment, and academically she was struggling. Juliette was sure this girl was in great hands, and recommended a great tutor, and also a speech therapist.

"Thank you so much," said Adam and Carrie over and over again.

"Thank you for your hospitality!"

"No need to thank us!"

"Okay I will stop by and see you again in one year! Please call me if you have any concerns."

"Alright, thank you. See you then!" The couple said with the daughter waving out the window goodbye,

Now *that* girl was in great hands.

●●●

Juliette could not get Jonathan off of her mind. His little bruised face. She knew for a fact he had been beaten. She had to go get a closer look as to what it was like when she wasn't there. She grabbed her keys off of the end table by the door and left her apartment. She was close to the house. She parked half mile away from it. As she approached it there was some light in the kitchen, she went to go get a closer look. She knew she could get in trouble for trespassing, and that was going beyond what she was supposed to do, but something compelled her.

She could hear the mom yelling but couldn't make out the words. She finally managed to make out a few of her slurred words.

"You are a worthless piece of junk! I should get rid of you now!"

That was enough for her.

Juliette looked past Madison to see the heavy-set Jack, passed out on the couch with a bottle of whisky in his hands.

Johnny was standing there as his mom was cursing at him, crying. Streams of tears ran down his cheeks.

What four year old should have to go through this?

Juliette picked up her cell phone and dialed 911. "New York police department what's your emergency?"

"Send police over here, a child is getting abused! I'm on the corner of Stonewood and Maple!"

"Okay we will send some officers over to your position now. Would you like me to stay on the line?"

"No, that's fine just hurry!"

Click.

As Juliette continued to watch, Madison picked up her fist and dropped it on the boys head with force. He fell to the floor. She walked out of the room stumbling, and came back with a wooden spoon.

She raised her arm holding the spoon and threw it down into the boy's stomach.

I can't let this kid get beaten until the police get here!

Juliette took a deep breath. She knew she had to go in there to save the little boy.

She walked over to the back screen door and pulled it open silently. Now she could hear everything very clearly. Madison landed one more blow to the boy's side before Juliette took action.

She ran in yelling at the top of her lungs. Madison, caught by surprise just stared at her, holding the spoon in her hands. Juliette ran up to the boy as fast as possible, pushed Madison hard to the floor, and grabbed the boy.

"You can't do that! It's... Kidnapping! I will find you and I promise I will kill you and Johnny!"

Juliette heard the words, but she didn't have time to think about it. She knew the police were coming soon. She ran out of the house, with the boy in her arms. A police car pulled up to the curb.

"Officers my name is Juliette. I'm the one who called you. The boy was being beaten inside this house, and I couldn't just watch the boy get hurt like that, so I ran in and grabbed him away from his parents."

The officer directed two more officers toward the house.

Juliette filed her report with the police, and watched as Johnny's parents were arrested. First Madison came out handcuffed. She looked at Juliette and growled. Jack followed. He was so intoxicated he tripped on his way out and fell to the floor, not moving. They had to pick the big man up and help him walk to the car. It was things like this that made Juliette worry about the kids she worked with. She had to fight to keep from being paranoid about the homes the children go to. She needed to rely on God to do this part of her job. She couldn't face these things alone. But she knew God was with her, and that he used her to help these kids. Again, a lesson in faith.

The officer offered to drive her to her car a half mile away, but she declined the offer. She needed time to think.

She saw Johnny being taken away on a stretcher. He looked at her with sad eyes on a bloodied face.

"I still see you?"

"Yes! I will visit you, I will see you!"

What would possess someone to beat this child?

They rolled the boy away and put him into an ambulance. Juliette walked to her car and drove home. She had much to think about that night.

●●●

Juliette was very eager to see little Johnny first thing in the morning. She called in and found out the address of the hospital where Jonathon had been taken. *I can't believe this!* Jonathon's hospital was the same hospital as her dad!

She could visit them both in one trip.

●●●

Johnny sat on the stretcher in the hospital, moaning. He was scared. He had lost a good deal of blood, and he felt a lot of pain in his head. The doctor came in and examined him, and he looked at the nurse and asked her something. Johnny could barely hear what they were saying.

"Excuse me, excuse me…"

"Yes John?" the doctor replied.

"Am I die?"

The doctor knew this little boy was scared. He got choked up and just looked into Jonathon's eyes. He made the mistake of not answering the boy.

Jonathon's eyes started to water.

●●●

Ethan heard rustling around. Dr. Hanserd entered his room.

"Hello Mr. Monroe"

"Doctor, I would like you to give me a truthful status report."

"You want the truth Ethan?"

"Yes. I know it's not good."

"You're right, it's not good. Your muscle functions are decreasing rapidly. Ethan, you may not have much time left." Ethan's body ached in sadness, but his heart leapt for joy. He was going home to his Father. But the one verse still got to him. He wanted to make sure before he passed away, that he realized what it meant when Paul said *"to live is Christ"*. Life was that good. Ethan knew it was something God wanted him to understand.

"Doctor... May I see a sheet of paper, envelope, and stamp please? I need to send one more letter."

"Yes, of course."

The Doctor leaned over and told the nurse. She left the room to retrieve the materials. It was most likely the last letter Ethan would send.

●●●

Juliette opened the door to the hospital and walked over to the front desk. There stood a short, stocky lady with red bushy hair, probably in her late 50's.

"Hello, can you tell me what room Jonathon Prickler is in?" The nurse's fingers moved rapidly across the computer keyboard.

"He is in room 506."

"Thank you so much."

Juliette was on her way to see the little boy who she had not been able to get out of her mind; the one who wanted to see her again because she was nice to him.

She opened the door. Although Juliette tried not to, she winced as she saw him. She quickly walked over to the nurse in the corner of the room facing away from John.

"Why is the gash in Jonathon's head getting bigger?" The nurse looked away for a second.

"It's... it's not. It is very infected, and if the infection keeps on spreading, it could reach the brain. This is a dangerous condition."

"What? Isn't there a way to stop the spreading?"

"We are doing the best that we can. He is on very strong antibiotics."

Juliette turned and faced little John. His eyes locked on her, he gave a smile. She walked over to his bed and sat down on the chair next to him. At first he stared at her, and then he reached down with his hand and grabbed her arm. His sweet eyes looked at her with trust, and her heart melted. Water was gathering in her eyes.

He asked her the same question he asked the doctor. She reached over and brushed his hair with her fingers.

"You will be just fine Johnny, just fine."

More tears were welling up in her eyes now, hoping her answer to his question was true.

"I will be back very soon to see you again okay? I have to do something now."

He looked at her with his soft eyes.

"Okay."

It was hard for her to leave, but she finally walked out of the room, on her way to see Ethan.

Knock knock

"Dad? Hello?"

Ethan could see Juliette's silhouette. The door opened and he could see Juliette's face smiling wide but with the tears still remaining from the visit with Jonathon.

"Sweetie, how is my lit-"

He began to lurch into a huge coughing fit. It scared her.

"Dad? Dad!?"

He was coughing even more now. The nurse rushed over to him. She looked over at Juliette

"I am going to have to ask you to leave, I am very sorry."

"You can't kick me out! This is my father!"

"We are not allowed to have any visitors here when he has an episode ma'am."

"This can't be happening! Dad!"

She began into a sob now. She was losing him. They led her out of the room. She sat on the tile floor outside of his room for the rest of the night.

●●●

Ethan heard his daughter weeping outside the room. He thought about the verse, "to live is Christ."

Does that mean if I live I can study God's word? Or maybe it means there's reason to live; it's a blessing to live. But what's the blessing to me on this earth? I'm a sick old man.

It then struck him like a brick to the face. Ethan leaned over and grabbed a piece of paper. He prayed, and then he began to write. . He wrote until he had filled four pages, and without even reading it over, he took the envelope and addressed it. He looked at the nurse to his side.

"Can you please send this letter for me? It is urgent."

"Of course," she gave him a smile.

The morning came without one minute of sleep; Ethan needed to talk to Juliette. He looked over; the clock read 7:43. Ethan slowly lifted himself to a sitting-up position. He waited there thirty minutes for Juliette. Then finally the beautiful brunette walked into the room.

"Just look at you" Ethan said in a serious voice, but with a smile.

"Dad? Is something wrong?"

"Honey, sit down."

I can't do this! How do I tell my own daughter I am going to die soon?

Ethan, still smiling, had a tear in his eye, then two. Juliette sat down and looked at him with a concerned face.

"Juliette. I am trying my hardest to make it through this. I want to be with my little girl. But you must understand all things come to an end. And-"

"Dad, don't."

"Honey, please let me..." He swallowed with difficulty, and took a few breaths. "Let me finish... If I don't make it, I will be with the Lord in heaven; you shouldn't have a reason to be burdened. When you were small, in the car on the way to your mother's funeral, I began to cry. You looked up at me with your sweet eyes and you told me 'Daddy, everything will be okay.' I want you to have that same strength in the possibility of my death." He began to take deep breaths again.

"Please! You can't leave!"
Juliette was crying.

"You have to remember, I will see you again in heaven!"

"So you are just going to leave me? Leave me here alone?"

"This is nothing I can control. You know I have been all over the world teaching to churches about what God did in our lives. This is where my story ends sweetie. My story is almost over. That doesn't mean yours has to. Keep on going with your ministry! Tell them about God, and how much He loves them."

"Dad, I love you." She threw her arms around him. Ethan's light blue hospital shirt was wet from his tears.

"Juliette, I love you too."
The coughing began again; she could hear it was getting harder for him to breathe. He was coughing so hard his body was shaking. She reached up and hugged him tight. She lost track of the time. When she looked up, he was asleep.

●●●

Dr. Hanserd was in the operating room performing surgery on Jonathon. They were trying to cut the infected area of the wound out. It should have been a fairly simple task, but if it didn't work, the infection could spread and Jonathon would die.

The doctors and nurses worked in silence. Dr. Hanserd wiped the blood off his gloves onto a clean rag and continued. The process took about 40 minutes to get rid of all of the infection. After the surgery concluded, they dressed the wound with a large white bandage on his head.

When he woke up, he was still in tremendous pain. He had been through more than any 4 year old should have to endure.

●●●

Juliette was leaning against Ethan crying. Resting her head on his shoulder, she finally fell asleep on the rough blanket covering Ethan. She could see that his movements were becoming slower, with heavier breathing and more labored swallowing.

Ethan started violent twitching. His face was expressionless, shaking. She looked up, and gave a loud scream.

"Somebody help!" The nurse ran and got the Doctor. The heart monitors *beeping* grew irregular. Juliette's heart sank.

A doctor ran in, instructing the nurse to take Juliette out of the room.

"That's my dad! You can't take me away! Please!" The nurse had to pry her away from that room.

"I am really sorry ma'am; please we will do what we can."

Juliette stood out of the room trying to look into the tinted glass. She just saw blurry shapes, but she saw the doctor performing CPR on Ethan. The doctor slowly turned his head towards the nurse. Juliette couldn't handle it. She began to slam on the door.

"Please, let me in! That's my father!"

The nurse walked over to the door and opened it.

"Ms. Monroe, I'm sorry." The nurse looked over to the bed Ethan laid on; the bed where the limp body was lying.

Juliette didn't breathe. She ran over to him crying out.

"Why, God? Why would you let this happen? He was my only family left!" She sobbed there until she had no more tears to cry. Her eyes felt dry. Even her heart felt dry. The feeling was unimaginable. Painful. Lonely.

She stared at his face, and the memories came flooding back. The time they went for ice cream after her violin, when they went to the theme park with her dad.

Oh how much he loved me!

She didn't know what to do next. She didn't know *why* God would let something like this happen. The last of her family had passed away, she was alone.

No, no. Don't be afraid.

She wasn't alone. She had God right beside her.

The next day…

Juliette's phone started ringing.
She picked it up, sniffing, and holding back the tears.

"He… Hello?"

"Juliette, it's Josh."

"Hey Josh."

"I am so sorry to hear about the loss, I really am."

"Thank you,"

"Can I please pray for you?"

"Yes, I would love that."

He said a prayer for her that she knew she would remember forever.

"Thank you, Josh."

"Don't thank me, it really is the least I could do."

"Oh Josh, the funeral is in three days."

"Is there anything I can do to help out with it? How about I have my wife bring the tapestry she's just finished? It can hang in the back or something."

Oh no! Why the tapestry? That thing looked hideous last I saw it!

"Umm, yeah, that would be fine."

She was against the idea, but didn't want to hurt Josh, or Hannah's feelings at all.

Three days passed…

They were setting up for the funeral, and it was almost ready to begin. Juliette was wearing her black skirt she hadn't worn for years, and her black button-up shirt.

She was anxious about the tapestry not in a good way. She didn't even want to look at it; it was just random colors with no specific beauty.

One thing she was excited about was that Josh said he had a word with the pastor, helping out with the message the pastor was going to say. She wanted the funeral to glorify God, and wanted people to know how much her dad had loved and trusted God even to the end.

Josh arrived carrying a rolled up tapestry. Juliette couldn't see what it was, and he had her close her eyes when he opened it up so he had time to put a blanket over it. She opened her eyes to an extremely large tapestry on the wall with a blanket covering it. She was nervous.

Juliette walked over to the front row and sat down. Staring at the casket in front of her, wishing so much it was empty, or all of it was just a dream, but it wasn't.

She looked at her cards with her eulogy on them, but threw them away. She wanted to give the speech by heart, from the heart.

The people gathered and silently sat down. The church was so full, there were people spilling into the hall. The funeral began with music and the pastors words, which seemed a bit like a blur. Then it was time to speak.

She got up and began.

"Thank you all for coming.

Almost all of you knew my father. It wasn't hard to see that he was a Godly man, and a loving man. He has changed my life in ways you couldn't believe. I hope his story is told many years to come. I know I am going to miss him, and I know you will too."

She shared a bit about his faith, his story, and his life. There was not a dry eye in the church. Many people nodded in agreement as they remembered Ethan.

She walked off, and then began to weep. She sobbed the rest of the funeral.

The pastor got up and began to speak.

"Many times we don't know why God does things the way he does. Many times we look at his plan and think *'this isn't right'* or *'why would He do that?'* We don't see the big picture though. We see one side of the story. When we look at the back of a tapestry, is it necessarily pretty? No."

He walked over and took the blanket off of the tapestry.

It's... it's... Hideous! Of course she didn't say it, for that would be rude, and even if not her mind was still on Ethan. But... it WAS hideous! Random colors and knots here and there, no specific design. Then the pastor continued:

"To our eyes, this is what Gods plan looks like sometimes. Random. Something doesn't look quite right, and we wonder why it looks that way. When I heard about Ethan's death I was devastated. I wondered *why*. But I wasn't seeing the big picture. Even though we see Gods plan sometimes as 'that doesn't make sense,' God sees the big picture."

The pastor carefully flipped the tapestry over, and Juliette gasped! It was one of the most beautiful things she had ever seen.

"While we see the back of God's plan, God sees it all. God knows why He does what He does, although we may not know, we may not realize the good that can come out of it. God does. He sees the front of the tapestry. He understands His plan."

Juliette's eyes were opened wide. She was astounded at the beauty of the tapestry, and that she had only seen the 'back' of Gods plan. She had not understood the reasons for so many of the things God had done in her life. She was crying hard now, her shoulders shaking from crying. *How could I have questioned? God used everything for a purpose.* She could see that as clearly as the beautiful design in this tapestry.

The pastor whispered something to Juliette then walked back up to the podium.

"There was a letter sent to me this week by a man from Ethan's past. This man did not know God most of his life, but realized that God forgave and welcomed him with open arms. This letter is about his transformation. It was sent to me from prison. This man's name is Cale. It's Ethan's brother. Ethan not only saved Juliette's physical life, but God used him to save Cale's spiritual life. In this letter Cale thanks Ethan for showing him what had been in front of his eyes the whole time, and he thanks Ethan for forgiving him and modeling God's grace to him. Cale described a beautiful letter he received from Ethan this past week. A letter of love, forgiveness, and full of the message of the gospel. Another thread in the tapestry.

The pastor then read the four page letter. The majority of the people in the church were weeping, and crying.

As soon as the funeral ended, Juliette stood by the door, thanking people as they left. It reminded her of her mom's funeral, staring up at her dad, who was crying from the loss of his wife.

Everyone was gone, except for her peace. That remained.

Two years later...

Juliette was sitting in the office of her three story house.

"Hey Johnny! Can you bring me my book?"

"Yes mom!" He hurried downstairs and grabbed Juliette's rough draft of her book, titled <u>Tapestry.</u> He ran back into the office, and handed her the draft.

"Thanks honey," she reached down and kissed him on his head, then rubbed his head with her hand, feeling his hair through her fingers.

She had adopted Jonathon.

Juliette knew she was blessed, to have the mom and dad she did, to have the son she did, with a job she enjoyed. The week of her father's death was so difficult, but she was only looking at the back of the tapestry. Ethan had shown her and taught her everything she knew. Juliette made sure his story was told, and that it would be told many years to come.

She grabbed Jonathon's hand.

"How'd you like to play a board game, sweet boy?"

He looked back at her with a sparkle in his eyes and smiled.